Playing Dirty

Book Two in the Action! Series

Playing Dirty

Book Two in the Action! Series

By G.A. Hauser

Linden Bay Romance, LLC
577 Mulberry Street, Suite 1520
Macon GA 31201

Playing Dirty
Book 2 of the Action! Series
Copyright © 2009: G.A. Hauser
Cover art by Beverly Maxwell
ISBN eBook: 978-1-60202-166-2
ISBN Trade paperback: 978-1-60202-167-9

First Linden Bay electronic publication: February 2009

Chapter One

Wearing black jeans, a black shirt, black tie, and back suit jacket, new young cable television heartthrob Keith O'Leary waited backstage at *Oprah* for his introduction. Hearing his name shouted on stage, the AD directed him to go.

Keith felt a mix of excitement and nervousness. His first job acting in a number one hit show had propelled him into the spotlight instantly. The only problem was...he was playing a gay character. And that character just happened to be in love with Carl Bronson, Keith's co-star and secret lover.

What had begun as two straight actors playing a romantic part had morphed into a reality that both Keith and Carl were trying to deal with. Being an out gay actor in Hollywood certainly had its pitfalls. And Keith's agent, Adam Lewis, continuously warned him to be very careful.

With all the internal dialogue spinning through his head from Adam to "deny, deny, deny", Keith felt confident he could keep his private life private, and his professional composure no matter the accusation. He had to. His career depended on it.

He jogged through the curtains to Oprah as they played the theme music for his hit show. Shaking her hand, he waved to the audience and smiled as they cheered wildly.

"Keith O'Leary, ladies and gentlemen! Keith O'Leary!"

Bowing, smiling broadly, Keith couldn't believe the screams from the females in the audience. He was coaxed to have a seat and the noise level finally settled down.

"Well! How does it feel to be the newest rising star on television?"

"Wonderful." Keith smiled as more cheers rang out.

"Obviously, you already have many fans."

"I know! Thank you!" He waved at the audience.

"Your first starring role, your first season, how are you coping with it all?"

"It's overwhelming. But I love it." Keith felt calmer now that he was sitting and talking. The anticipation was worse than the reality.

"Were you hesitant to star as a gay man who is out?"

"No. I enjoy the challenge. I think the show helps to examine alternative lifestyles in a positive way."

Shrieking cheers emerged from the crowd.

"I think many of the ladies are jealous you get to kiss that handsome co-star."

Keith blushed and smiled. "I bet!"

"Is he as nice in person as he seems to be on TV?"

"He's great. Yes. Carl Bronson is a very nice guy."

"Did that fact make it easier for you?"

"Yes. Of course." Keith couldn't wipe the smile from his face.

"Do you get many fan letters from gay men? Thanking you for your support?"

"Not yet. But I assume I will. I'm happy to bring to light a character who can show he's not afraid to love a man. I think too much energy is wasted on ignorance and preventing gay marriage."

"I agree!"

Keith smiled as the audience clapped in support.

"Tell us what else you do. What are your hobbies?"

As Keith talked about his life, he knew things would work out. It all felt right.

~

Carl wanted to go with Keith and wait backstage but, wisely, he didn't. The last thing either of them wanted to do was verify the already growing suspicion that he and Keith were real lovers. There was no way Carl was ready for that. He wanted a long career on television and especially in films. Unfortunately, out gay men did not get leading roles in romance or action movies. Not to his knowledge anyway.

Reading the new script, waiting for Keith to come home, Carl daydreamed about a time when the men in Hollywood wouldn't have to hide what they did. They weren't there yet. But soon. Maybe soon.

As he heard a key turning the lock of the door, his heart lit on fire. Standing from his position on the couch, he waited for his first glance of the man he adored.

Seeing him come through the door and beaming, Carl knew Keith had done just fine. "Come here, baby."

Keith tossed his keys aside and hugged Carl tight. "I love you."

"I love you too, Keith." Carl crushed him in his embrace and kissed his neck.

~

"Yes, hello, remember me? I called you last week about the relationship between Carl Bronson and Keith O'Leary."

"Yes. I remember. Do you have anything else we can use?"

"I will soon. How would you like evidence of their relationship?"

"We'd love it. What do you have in mind?"

"A videotape of them together, making love."

"Oh?"

"I just want to know if I went to the trouble of getting it, you would use it."

"Are you kidding? Yes. We'll use it. And we'll pay you very well for it."

"I thought so. Good. I'll be in touch with you soon."

"Great. I'll be waiting."

Chapter Two

Talent agent Adam Lewis stood at the check-out line at the grocery store with his attorney lover, Jack Larsen. Once he'd loaded the conveyer belt with their selections, he paused and read the headlines on the sleazy tabloid papers that sat in the rack nearby.

"Oh shit."

"What?" Jack asked, standing behind their cart.

Adam picked up the paper and flipped pages until he came to the article he was interested in.

"Adam?"

Looking up at Jack's concerned expression, Adam sighed, "It's about Keith O'Leary and Carl Bronson."

"And?"

"It says they're real life lovers. Jack, Keith will be so upset when he sees this."

Jack tilted his head to the check-out girl who was beginning to scan their items. Adam set the paper on top of their groceries to purchase.

Feeling sick to his stomach, knowing the conversations he'd had with Keith about how to react to the assumptions and interview questions, Adam hoped the tabloids wouldn't go too far in their accusations. But it seemed they already had. Waiting until their groceries were bagged and paid for, Adam picked the paper back up and read the rest of the article while Jack pushed the cart beside him.

"How bad is it?" Jack asked as he unlocked the trunk of their car.

"Bad. Very bad."

"What the hell does it say?" Jack shifted the groceries over.

"It says, 'A source close to the one of the men claims that the steamy romance portrayed by the adorable Keith O'Leary and handsome Carl Bronson, (acting as Dennis Jason and Troy Wright on *Forever Young*) is more than just an act. The two men have shacked up in Bronson's condo in Santa Monica and are in the midst of a passionate love affair.'"

Jack shut the trunk and pushed the cart away. When he returned he sat behind the wheel of his Jaguar as Adam climbed into the passenger seat.

"Jack, I'm really worried about how Keith will react to this when he hears about it."

"What are you supposed to do about it?" Jack started the car.

"I should get him a publicist and get these rumors quashed."

"They're not rumors, Adam." Jack pulled out of the parking spot.

"I know. But it'll kill his career. Once *Forever Young* is through, their futures as leading men will be too."

"Don't be so pessimistic. It can't really be that bad for actors who come out."

"Oh? Name one."

"What?" Jack asked.

"Name one actor who has come out of the closet that is a big name in movies or TV."

"Uh…"

"I rest my case." Adam folded the paper and took out his mobile phone.

"You're calling him now?"

"I have to. What choice do I have?" Adam felt Jack's hand on his leg to comfort him. "Keith? Adam Lewis."

"Hello, Adam."

"Have you happened to have seen this week's *Inspirer*?"

"No. Why?"

Adam clasped Jack's hand tightly. "There's an article about you and Carl living together."

"Already? How the hell did they figure it out? I've just moved in."

"It says there's a source close to one of you. Any idea who that could be?"

"No. But I'm going to find out."

"Look, in the meantime, let me hire you a publicist who can squash these rumors or at least battle them."

"Okay, Adam. Whatever you say."

"I'm afraid you'll have to appear on someone's talk show soon proclaiming your love for a woman. Just don't jump on a couch when you do."

"Come on, Adam. Can't I just say Carl and I are good friends? Carl even suggested we say we're living together because we're going green and carpooling."

Adam cracked up. Jack turned to look at him curiously. "I love it."

"Well?"

"Give it a try. Who knows?"

"Thanks for the heads up, Adam."

"No problem, Keith. And I will get you a publicist."

"Okay."

"I'll talk to you soon." Adam hung up and smiled despite his fears.

"So?" Jack asked.

"He took it well. But he's in trouble, Jack. Big trouble."

Jack raised Adam's hand to his lips to kiss.

Sighing sadly, Adam wished everyone could be as lucky as he and Jack were and not have to hide their true feelings.

~

"What did he say?" Carl asked when Keith hung up.

"He said there's an article in the new weekly rag that outs us."

"Implies we're gay? Or?"

"No. Some 'source' says we're lovers and living together."

"What source?" Carl set the script they were rehearsing down and closed the gap between them.

"You don't think Charlotte would let something like that leak out to boost ratings do you?"

"How the heck would she figure out we were living together already?"

"Spies?" Keith wrapped around Carl and held him tight.

"This sucks. I didn't think we'd be dealing with this so quickly." Carl rubbed Keith's back in comfort.

"Adam's hiring me a publicist. Maybe you should speak to the guy as well." Keith leaned back so he could see Carl's green eyes. The heat of Carl's body was already making him excited.

"I should. I'll call my agent and see what he thinks."

Keith dug his hand into Carl's thick, brown hair. "I wish we could just be honest."

"We've had this discussion before, Keith. We can't."

"I know." Keith urged Carl from behind to kiss him. At the touch of their lips, Keith knew their relationship was worth fighting for. Their careers shouldn't have to be sacrificed for it. Others had kept hidden in the closet for years. Somehow, they would manage to keep the wolves at bay.

~

Carl lost himself on Keith's tongue. As it entered his mouth, he felt burning rushes of pleasure all over his body. He and Keith had only recently begun acting in a show together as gay lovers. But the non-acting part of their relationship was even more recent. It was a case of reality imitating art. As their characters Dennis and Troy's passion was emblazoned on the screen in *Forever Young*, he and Keith's love had blossomed.

Hearing those luscious, whimpering moans of Keith's when he was hungry for sex, Carl tightened his grip around Keith's body and began grinding his hips against Keith's. When their erections pressed together, Carl felt his skin erupt with chills. The learning of their new lines had to be put on hold once again.

Carl couldn't get enough of Keith and it appeared Keith felt the same about him. The craving to be naked and penetrating each others' bodies was so strong it was consuming.

Digging his hand into Keith's soft, blond hair, Carl deepened the already steaming kiss, opening his mouth wider receiving Keith's tongue which felt as erect as his dick at the moment.

Keith pulled Carl's shirt out of his jeans, reaching his hands under it to touch his skin. His respirations rising in depth and speed, Carl broke the kiss to gasp for air and pressed his face into Keith's neck to gnaw on it hungrily.

"Bed…bedroom…now." Keith arched his back and thrust his hips against Carl's.

Carl didn't want to stop what they were doing. He dug his hand into Keith's jeans and searched for his cock. Finding it had grown hard down the leg of his pants, Carl pulled his hand out and opened Keith's zipper for better access.

"Oh, God…" Keith groaned in agony. "Bed! Now!"

Carl released Keith's hard-on from his tight jeans, running his palm along it. "You fantastic mother-fucker." Carl began urging them to the bedroom, still connected, still kissing and fondling.

When they drew closer to the bed, Keith tilted back to pull his shirt over his head.

Carl crouched down and licked Keith's cock.

"Augh!" Keith growled. "Naked! Bed! Now!"

Trying not to laugh at Keith's urgent tone, Carl gave Keith's cock a last long, wet lap before he stood back and frantically stripped off his clothing.

Stepping out of his jeans and socks, Carl started working on his shirt buttons as Keith leaned down and slipped Carl's cock into his mouth. "Ah!" Carl gasped feeling Keith's deep, wet heat. "Bed! Now!" he echoed Keith's earlier plea.

It made Keith crack up with laughter and Carl's cock dropped out of his mouth when he did.

Grabbing Keith around the waist, Carl picked him up and dove with him onto the king-sized mattress. The minute they were horizontal, Carl began squirming on Keith's body, trapping it under him.

"Fuck me. Fuck me," Keith breathed between kisses, bending his knees and spreading his legs.

Unable to calm his pulse or urges, Carl scrambled to reach for the lube and condoms in the nightstand drawer.

As Keith waited impatiently, he hissed, "Do we need rubbers, Carl? Do we really need rubbers?"

"I don't know. I can't think right now. Ask me again later." Carl rolled one on and slathered lube all over it. Once he was ready, Carl pushed Keith's legs back against Keith's chest and pressed his dick into that waiting hole.

"I can't jack off like this," Keith complained.

"Tough. Wait." Carl jammed his cock into Keith, rocking Keith back.

Keith grabbed Carl's face and tried to contort himself to reach his lips. When he couldn't accomplish that either, he started urging Carl, "Come. Come in me. Come…"

Carl felt his skin cover with chills. He thrust in deeper, faster, feeling his body rush with pleasure. Just as it began to overwhelm him, he opened his eyes and stared down into Keith bright blue irises. Shuddering as he came, Carl clenched his teeth and arched his back to get even deeper, balls deep.

"That's it, baby..." Keith panted. "That's it."

Astounded at how intense the orgasms were with Keith, Carl took a few moments to come back to earth before he could function. Sweat ran down his temple to his neck, tickling his skin. Feeling slightly recuperated from the climax, Carl inched away, freeing Keith's legs from their locked position. As he did, he pulled out, removing the rubber and dropping it gently to the carpet.

Once Keith extended his legs, moaning at the relief of being released from the cramped position, Carl wedge himself between Keith's thighs and drew Keith's entire cock into his mouth.

They had become so comfortable, so attuned to each other's needs, Carl savored the chance at tasting Keith's come. Not long ago it was strange, intimidating, to touch a man in those taboo places, to taste the sweetness of his seed. Not now. Now it was natural and wonderful, and Carl craved it like air.

~

With the vibrating echoes of Carl's cock in his ass, Keith savored being inside Carl's hot, wet mouth. No longer did Carl recoil at the possibility of Keith shooting into it. Carl appeared to hanker for a taste of Keith on a daily basis.

They had become so close, so confident. Literally from timid touches to deep fucking and sucking, they had grown to enjoy the taste and touch of each other in so many ways. Keith no longer felt it was odd, uncomfortable, or awkward to reach out and stroke his lover's dick, push his fingers inside his ass, lick his skin all over his body. The days of fear and anxiety about holding each others' dicks and the terror over the stigma of being gay, in private, were over, replaced by self-assurance and the desire to please in the bedroom.

Keith purred a deep, contented sound as Carl drew him into his mouth to the root, running his teeth lightly over his skin and his tongue tracing down his length. As Keith began to rise with the climax, Carl slid his finger inside Keith's slick back passage, massaging his prostate with light, gentle strokes that made Keith go insane.

A prelude to the explosion shivered through Keith's body. Keith wished he could hold back and prolong the splendid blowjob, but the urge to come was too powerful.

As Carl worked his finger deeper into Keith's ass, Keith let loose a howl of pleasure, tensing his back muscles and feeling the shiver down to his toes. Throbbing, rocking into Carl's throat, Keith gave up his seed and soared with the aftershocks as Carl sucked him down, draining him and milking him with his hand.

Choking for breath, Keith moaned in exquisite agony, sated, madly in love, and astonished at the depth of the emotional attachment he and Carl had developed. It was the most incredibly experience in his life. Add to that the fact that he was starring in his first hit cable television drama in a career move of a lifetime. He had never been happier.

Finally able to open his eyes and breathe normally, Keith looked down to see Carl lapping at his cock leisurely. Carl's eyes were closed, his concentration solely on his task of getting every drop of come out of Keith's dick.

When Carl seemed to have his fill, his long, dark eyelashes raised revealing his emerald eyes.

"Get over here," Keith prompted, reaching out his hands.

Carl's wicked smile appeared as he crawled up Keith's body to his lips. Keith cupped Carl's face and tasted his own come on Carl's mouth. Pausing for a breath, Keith whispered, "I love you."

Carl smiled as he replied, "I love you too, Keith." After some sweet gentle kissing, Carl said, "But…we have to learn the new script."

"I know." Keith pushed Carl's dark brown hair back from his

dewy forehead.

"Let's wash up."

"Okay." Keith gave in, though all he wanted to do was snuggle.

~

Once they had rinsed off and dressed, Keith found the scripts. As he read his, he recalled Adam's conversation. Though he and Carl had been distracted by their love making, inevitably, they had to admit there was a problem that they needed to address. It was just in the heat of the moment they had a chance to pretend they didn't have any worries. Pretend. That was what he and Carl did best. They were actors. They were only playing gay characters on TV. Right? Isn't that what the viewing public really needed to hear? *We aren't gay; we're straight. We just play the part of gay men.*

The irony to Keith was their popularity. The amount of fan sites on the internet that ran video clips of their sexual encounters on screen was growing. Not only gay men were setting up these sites. Women were too. Millions of women across the globe were going mad for the sex scenes of Dennis Jason and Troy Wright. Why, then, did the reality of two men being gay scare the bejesus out of the producers?

It was the worst case of hypocrisy Keith could ever imagine. And it wasn't fair to him and Carl. Why was it if they chose to come out to the public that their heterosexual acting roles would vanish? Why?

That was a question that continued to plague Keith. Ironically, he already knew. He couldn't even admit he was gay to his parents. How would he admit he was gay to the public? No. That could never happen. And like his trusted "gay" agent Adam Lewis had advised, "deny, deny, deny".

"Carl?"

"Yes, babe?" Carl returned from the kitchen with two glasses of wine.

"Thanks." Keith took his and sipped it, setting it on a coaster on the coffee table. "What are we going to do? Should I move out?"

"Fuck no. I thought we were going to say something about being green. Why don't you trust me on that? It's the new catchphrase of 2008. Green. We're green. Carpooling."

"You really think anyone will buy it?"

"We have to make them buy it." Carl drank his wine, placing the glass down next to Keith's. "What exactly did Adam Lewis say?"

"He said he found an article in the rags that exposed us."

"Rags. Hello? No one believes those idiots. Don't worry. You're not moving out." Carl picked up the script. "What perversion were we rehearsing?"

"You suck my dick." Keith grinned wickedly.

"Uh huh. Sure I do. Oh, here it is. We go to a gay nightclub and dance together. How bold!"

"I know. Dennis and Troy are fearless."

"I wonder what Charlotte has in mind for that scene. You think she'll really have a gay nightclub for us to go to? Or some pathetic stage set with a few man dancing in the shot?"

"You're asking me? You're the pro. I'm the new guy." Keith took another sip of wine.

"If I know Charlotte, we'll be shooting at the hottest gay dance club in LA ."

"Really?" Keith felt excited at the idea. How weird was that, when the notion of gay anything a few months ago would have scared him to death?

"She's pretty determined to have realistic shoots. Remember the first season? When Omar and Cheryl's character were courting? She went to Paris and shot their romance scenes there."

"Yes. That's right. I do remember." Keith smiled at the thought. "We should ask her."

"No!" Carl nudged Keith's knee. "Don't you dare. If you ask her if we're shooting in a gay bar, she'll think you want to. No. Just keep quiet and we'll just see how it goes."

Keith put his glass down and sat up on the couch. "Carl. Do you think Charlotte is capable of planting the seed of our love being real into the tabloids?"

After a long moment, Carl sighed. "Yes. I wouldn't put it past her."

"Should we ask? Confront her?"

"I don't know."

"There must be a way of doing that without tipping her off."

"How?"

"Let me think about it."

"Just run it by me first."

"I will."

"Now, where were we?" Carl raised the script to eye level.

As Keith thought about everything, he struggled to come up with a way of asking Charlotte if she was the "source" or not.

Chapter Three

Carl had his face in the script while they descended the elevator to his car. Keith seemed to be able to memorize his lines easily while he struggled. At the lobby level, Keith tapped Carl's arm to alert him they had arrived at their floor, and exited the elevator with him to the parking garage door. Before they left the lobby, Carl heard some noise at the entrance and paused to look back. A group of photographers were gathered just outside, shoving their lenses at them, flashes going off like mad.

Carl froze where he stood. "You have got to be kidding me."

"Holy shit, Keith gasped. "What do you want to do, Carl?"

"I want to confront them. I just don't know if I have the damn balls."

One began banging on the glass, shouting for Carl and Keith to talk to them.

As if that comment forced Keith to come to a decision, he stormed over to the mob and did the unthinkable. He allowed the feral pack of paparazzi in.

"How long have you men been dating?"

"Is your sexual attraction in reality what makes the sex scenes in *Forever Young* so believable?"

"Are you coming out for yourselves or the show's ratings?"

Keith held up his hands to quiet them. "Hello? Can I say something?"

Carl felt his throat close up. Although he had wanted this

kind of attention from the media all his life, he didn't like what they were exposing.

"Now," Keith shouted, finally getting a chance to speak, "Carl and I are friends. Period. Though I know you vultures would love the story to be different, it isn't. I'm pretty strapped for cash at the moment and living here is helping me financially." When they broke into a loud rebuttal of questions, he silenced them again. "Be quiet and let me finish!" In the pause, he added, "We're both very environmentally conscious and the price of gas has gone through the roof. It just made sense to commute together and economize. I know you want to hear something else. But it's not happening between us. We're friends. Emphasis on the word 'friends'!"

Carl watched the men's faces as Keith gave it his best shot. The doubt in their expressions was very obvious.

"Both Carl Bronson and I are straight. There is no question about that. Okay? So, whoever is giving you the opposite information either wants to harm our careers or is just hoping we're a couple for the sake of ratings. Enough said on the topic."

"Do you have girlfriends?"

"If you're straight, who are the ladies in your life?"

"Why are you so afraid to admit you're lovers?"

Carl cringed at the force of venom being spouted. He knew damn well the paparazzi only believed what was good for distribution numbers of the papers they sold pictures to.

"That's it. Good day, gentlemen." Keith nodded for Carl to go.

The pack of hungry hounds followed them all the way to Carl's garage. Shouting out more incriminating accusations, taking photo after photo, Carl suddenly understood the fear and anxiety that these types of encounters caused, and didn't wonder why so many celebrities reacted violently.

Locked in his Corvette, backing out of his garage, Carl bit his lip on his rage and imagined gunning the engine and running a few of them over. Once they had driven out of the parking area, Carl wiped the sweat off his forehead. "That sucked."

"Shit." Keith covered his eyes tiredly. "We are so fucked."

"I can't tell you how much I'm hating this."

"I know."

"You know the ironic part?" Carl asked sadly. "I used to crave being in front of a crowd like that. I imagined getting photographed wherever I went. To be in every entertainment magazine in the country. Now?" He choked at the irony. "I want to run and hide."

"We have to be seen with women, Carl. We have to."

"I know. But I'm not happy about it."

Keith reached for Carl's hand. "We'll get through it. Let's just make a game of it, okay?"

"A game?" Carl stopped for a red light and stared at Keith's handsome profile.

"Yes. If they think they're the only ones to play dirty, they're mistaken. Two can play it that way."

When the light changed, Carl hit the gas. "What way? What are you thinking?"

"Carl, you and I are going to double date."

"Why did I have a feeling you were going to say that."

As they pulled onto the studio lot, Carl showed the guard at the gate his ID.

"Adam said that they can arrange to get us a couple of women to be seen with."

"This sucks." Carl parked in a spot and shut the engine. Before they got out, Carl twisted to face Keith. "We barely have enough time to have fun together as it is, Keith, with our tight rehearsal schedule. When exactly are we going to find time to date women?"

"Twice a month? Be seen in some overcrowded restaurant in West Hollywood? I should think that would be enough."

Once they were out of the car and walking to the studio, Carl said, "And how do we stop those pretend girlfriends from going to the same lousy tabloids and selling their story? Keith, I don't like it."

Halting in his footsteps, Keith stared at Carl and replied, "I don't see what choice we have."

~

Inside the studio's wardrobe room, changing into his character's clothing, Keith eyed everyone around him with suspicion. Someone was talking to the press. It had to be one of the crew, Keith was convinced. He had no idea how they had found out he had moved in with Carl, but how hard could it be to deduct? They commuted in together now and exited from the same damn car.

His wardrobe assistant, Melvin, shifted hangers on a rack, handing Keith a shirt and a pair of slacks. When Mel caught Keith's eye, he asked, "What's wrong? Get up on the wrong side of the bed this morning?"

"What's that supposed to mean?" Keith took off his shirt and replaced it with the one Mel was handing to him.

"What's with the evil look?"

"What look?" Keith narrowed his eyes at him.

"Whatever!" Melvin threw up his hands and walked away.

Carl shook his head at Keith in admonishment, having overheard the conversation. Trying not to allow it to consume him, Keith continued to change his clothing, running over the lines in his head so he didn't forget them.

"Boys?"

He and Carl spotted their director, Charlotte Deavers, flagging them down. "A word?"

"What did we do now?" Carl breathed anxiously.

"Bet she read the article in the tabloid."

Charlotte held each of their hands and brought them to a private spot to whisper softly, "Have you seen that YouTube video yet?"

"YouTube?" Keith wasn't prepared for that.

"What are you talking about, Charlotte?" Carl's voice was deep and serious.

"One of my friends found a video on YouTube of that love scene we shot last week."

Keith was confused. "What the hell do you mean?"

Rubbing her face first as if gathering her thoughts, Charlotte replied, "Last week we shot a sex scene with four cameras around the bed. Remember?"

Carl spoke up, "Snippets for that two minute love scene?"

"Yes."

"When we were both naked?" Keith felt sick.

"That's the one."

"Now it's on YouTube?" Carl tilted his head. "You mean the finished copy?"

"No. Not the one we edited. It's a full length version of you two on the bed."

It was so shocking, Keith staggered back in terror. Carl caught him, holding him tight.

"Charlotte, that would mean someone who was filming it sent in the video, correct? One of your cameramen?"

Keith needed to vomit. He felt his skin go clammy and his stomach fill with ice.

"That's what I thought originally, Carl. But the video is amateurish. I think someone used their mobile phone or something."

"You have got to be kidding me!" Carl exclaimed. "Charlotte, you have to find out who did that and make them delete it."

The feeling had left Keith's legs. He needed to sit down or he would pass out. He remembered that scene. How could he not?

They were both nude, hard as a rock, and simulating oral and anal sex.

"Keith?" Carl grabbed him around the waist as Keith began to sink to the floor.

"Shit. Let me find a chair." Charlotte raced off.

"Keith, babe, take it easy." Carl held him up, embracing him. "We'll deal with it."

"Here." Charlotte set a folding chair near Keith. She helped Carl sit him down on it.

Keith was numb. Feeling as if he would pass out, he stuck his head between his knees and closed his eyes, hoping the sickness would subside. This was his worst nightmare. He and Carl, naked, having "sex" on the internet. Did it get any worse than that?

Carl crouched beside him, rubbing his back. "Charlotte, you need to do some investigating. Bring in an outside agency and figure it out. This is way out of line."

Charlotte knelt down and tried to get Keith to meet her eyes. "Sweetie? It's not that bad. Believe me. The viewers' comments are all positive. They completely support the two of you."

That angered him even more. Keith peered up at her face. "Ratings? Are you actually talking to me about viewer ratings when my life is falling apart?"

"It's not falling apart, sweet-stuff. Honest." She petted back his hair from his forehead. "It's all good. Believe me. Just roll with it. Roll with it and pretend it's all part of the nature of show business."

Keith showed his teeth in a snarl. "Is she kidding me, Carl?"

"No. I know what she's getting at, Keith." Carl sat on the dusty floor next to him. "We just have to play it cool. Like it's no big deal. If we freak or do something drastic, it'll confirm everyone's suspicions."

Charlotte whispered softly, "Are you guys lovers?"

"No!" Keith shouted.

"Okay. Take it easy. Everyone knows you're living together."

"Do they?" Carl asked, "Is that common knowledge?"

"Yes. You commute together every day. People aren't stupid, Carl." She stepped back. "Just don't sweat it. Okay? Look. I need to get you two back to work. Now, take another minute to compose yourselves and get back on the set."

After she walked away, Keith sat up in the chair. "I am so sick I feel like vomiting."

"We'll deal with this. Just inhale a few deep breaths."

"Why did she tell us this now? Huh? Before a taping? I'm a wreck."

"You have to straighten up, Keith. Don't show her you can't take the heat. Please."

Hearing that as a serious warning about not getting cut from the show and keeping his job, Keith rubbed the cool sweat off his face and stood. "Fine. Whatever. Let's go."

Carl's black slacks were dirty from sitting on the floor. As he slapped at them, Keith helped, brushing the dry dust from the material. Feeling Carl's solid legs under the thin fabric, Keith felt a flash of fire and stopped touching him instantly.

"Thanks." Carl didn't seem to notice anything unusual.

"Let's get today over with. I need a fucking drink." Keith nudged him to head back to the set.

"You can always hit Betty up for a snort."

Thinking about the older co-star who played Carl's character's mother, Keith actually smiled in amusement. "I should. But that whiskey she drinks is murder."

Carl chuckled softly, placing his arm around Keith's shoulders.

After Ken, their make-up man, brushed Keith's hair and powdered his shine, he and Carl stood by for the instructions.

Seeing everyone waiting, Keith knew it would take a supreme effort on his and Carl's part to act normal, pretend things were fine, and go through their lines.

But he and Carl had had this discussion before. They were the great pretenders now. Everything in their life was make-believe, except, Keith hoped, their love. If that wasn't real, then what good was all the agony?

"Okay, you boys ready?" Charlotte asked in her usual professional manner as if she hadn't just dropped an atomic bomb on them.

"Yes," they both replied softly.

"Living room scene. Take one. Action!"

Keith knew his line was first up. "A gay bar? Not really, Troy. How could we go to a gay bar?"

Carl reached for Keith's hand and squeezed it tight. "One fun night out to relax and be ourselves. What's the big deal?"

"The big deal?" Keith choked at the absurdity. "Your family is already giving us a hard time, and mine have no clue I'm gay. It is a big deal, Troy."

"Dennis," Carl cupped Keith's jaw gently, "it's a night where we don't have to hide. We can let our guard down and be ourselves."

Keith melted at Carl's gaze. He always turned to mush whether it was on or off camera. "Fine. A night at a gay bar. Okay."

"I love you. Come here." Carl wrapped around Keith and kissed him.

Instantly Keith imagined that evil culprit filming them with a small mobile phone or another device. He parted from Carl's mouth and struggled not to look around the crowded room.

"I just hope you know what you're doing, Troy."

"Don't worry."

"Famous last words." Keith reached for the front door on the set.

"Cut!"

Keith dropped his hand to his side and waited for the verdict.

"Well done. Go take a break."

Hearing Charlotte's approval, Keith walked over to the

refreshment table and poured himself a glass of juice.

"You okay?"

Meeting Carl's gaze, Keith shook his head. "No. I'm surprised she didn't make me redo that last scene. I have so much shit going on in my head at the moment I must look like I'm passing a kidney stone."

"Yes, but ironically it's the same expression your character should have."

"True." Keith sipped his juice. "I'm so sick about this, Carl."

"When we get back to my place we'll look up the site."

"Do we really want to do that?"

Carl poured coffee into a cup. "I do. I want to see whose YouTube site it belongs to. There has to be a way of figuring it out."

"You know the weird thing, Carl?"

"No, what?"

"I expected fan sites to pop up, even with gay overtones, considering our characters, but for someone to secretly video tape us squirming in bed? It's the worst violation of privacy I could imagine. Why couldn't they be satisfied with the two minute montage Charlotte would have provided? The one she edited for the show? Christ, Carl, how much do you want to bet they can see both our erections?"

"Stop. Honestly, Keith, I can't think about this now and work at the same time."

"I'm sorry, Carl." Keith beat himself up for moving in with Carl. It was a mistake. But now that they were living together, Keith didn't want them to be apart.

~

Another scene between two other cast members, Cheryl Jones and Omar Desmond acting as Doris and Xavier, who also played lovers, was shot quickly. As Keith waited for the next step in filming, he found the crew packing up. "Shit. She's really taking us on location for this."

"She is." Carl ran his fingers through his hair nervously.

"A real gay bar?" Keith asked.

"I don't know if it'll be gay, but it's obviously out somewhere."

Keith raced after his director before she slipped away. "Charlotte?"

"Yes, sugarplum?"

"Where's the shoot going to be?"

"At a bar in West Hollywood."

"A gay bar?"

"Yes. We needed the dancers. And the atmosphere is fantastic."

"Dancers?" Keith tried not so sound like a shocked hillbilly.

"You'll see." She kissed his cheek and waved her entourage on.

~

Sitting in the back of a chauffeur driven sedan, Carl leaned his elbow on the armrest on the door, gazing out at the traffic on Santa Monica Boulevard. He didn't want to talk to Keith about it. They didn't know the driver and everyone was on their list of suspects now.

When they were stopped at a roadblock, Carl leaned closer to the window to see the police had barricaded the city block off that held the popular gay club. Gawkers leered beyond the police line to get a glimpse of the stars involved in the shoot.

Rubbing the stubble on his jaw anxiously, Carl felt his stomach flip. He was going to be inside a gay bar. How easy would it be for their phantom photographer to claim the shots were from their real life and not the show? This was just too simple a game to play. They may as well throw up their hands and admit it after all the incriminating photographs hit the internet and tabloid press.

Carl looked over at Keith. He seemed pale and pinched, staring out of the opposite window.

The car stopped directly in front of the club. Carl couldn't read the name of the place until he got out and stood on the street in front of it. The area was chaotic with equipment, crew, and spotlights surrounding the entrance.

Carl felt Keith brush his side. When he looked down at him, Keith was riveted to the club. "Have you ever heard of it?"

"No. You?" Keith briefly met his eyes.

"No."

"Look at the flier in the window."

Carl scanned the façade and found it. "My Big Fat Dick Contest? Oh, for crying out loud."

"I had no idea places like this existed."

"Makes two of us."

"I swear, I'm so fucking nervous I can't remember any of my lines."

"We don't have many." Carl looked around for Charlotte. "If I remember right, we enter, dance, and kiss. Something like that."

"We have lines, Carl."

"A few. Don't worry." Although Carl reassured Keith, he was very anxious himself. Where was this plot going and how much more could they do to damage their acting reputation?

We'll never get another role after this show ends. We're completely finished.

"Okay, boys." Charlotte materialized out of thin air behind them. "Just the quick shot of you two entering. Holding hands. Then we go in. Okay?"

"Yeah, fine," Carl mumbled, petrified of what the inside of the place held in store for them.

She spun around and began hollering for the camera crew to get ready.

Keith nervously combed his fingers through his blond hair as he eyed the surroundings. "Look at all those spectators."

Carl turned to where he pointed. An enormous crowd was gathering behind the barricades. Cops stood between the wooden horses to prevent any breeching. When Carl faced them to get a better look, a loud squeal erupted from the women who began shouting and waving at them. "Our loyal fans."

"It's all women, Carl. That has to be a good thing."

"True. See? Don't lose hope." Carl waved back. Another roar of high-pitched screams ricocheted around them.

"Okay…" Charlotte looked back at the noise. "Oh, we need to shut them up." She scanned the employees who were rushing by them. "Bruce! Brucie!" She waved. "Get over there and quiet them down."

Bruce nodded and raced over to the raucous chaos.

"Let's get this done and get inside. The noise level out here is horrible."

"Our fans love us," Carl chuckled.

"They do! Believe me, I know," she laughed. "Grab hands. Let's go."

As she backed up, Carl reached out for his lover's hand. "You ready?"

"As I'll ever be." Keith connected to Carl's fingers and squeezed tight.

"Club entrance scene. Take one. Action!"

On cue, Carl began walking Keith up to the front of the club. He opened the door and just before he allowed Keith in, Keith gave his ass a good caress. Carl twisted around to see his demonic grin, shaking his head at him. Once they were inside, Carl sighed, "We'll have to do it again now."

"Wanna bet?" Keith didn't release his hand.

Seconds later Charlotte raced in breathlessly. "Nice touch,

Keith! I loved it."

"Told ya." Keith teased.

"You're beginning to get as demented as our director." Carl released Keith's grip and crossed his arms over his chest.

"Okay. Inside." Charlotte led the way into the main dance floor of the club.

When Carl pushed back the doors to follow her, the room went silent. As he and Keith entered, Carl found dozens of men, mute, staring at them. "Oh, my fucking God." Carl felt their curious intense gazes, most likely asking themselves, "Are they or aren't they?"

"Carl…"

"Easy, Keith. Inhale, exhale."

As Carl tried to smile amiably at the scores of men who watched them as they passed, he noticed buff male dancers in only g-strings, ogling as they approached. "Hey," Carl greeted a man as he walked by. "You all right?"

"What are you doing?" Keith hissed.

"They're staring at me," Carl whispered back. "What the hell am I supposed to do?"

"Okay, gentlemen!" Charlotte shouted to the men in the crowded room. "Just act naturally. Dance, drink, talk, be yourselves."

Melvin appeared out of nowhere. He reached out his hand. "Give me your jacket, Carl."

Carl removed his suit jacket, handing it to him. "You must be in heaven."

"I am. It's my favorite haunt." Mel folded the blazer over his arm. "Enjoy!"

"What are we supposed to do? Carl, my mind is blank."

"We dance." Carl noticed some of the men trying to listen. Speaking softer, Carl leaned to Keith's ear. "We dance like we're fucking each other, kiss and make out. Remember?"

"In front of all these gay guys?"

"Shut up." Carl couldn't feel any more nervous if he tried.

"I need a fucking drink," Keith announced.

To Carl's amazement, someone handed him one.

"What is it?" Keith asked the handsome man.

"Rum and Coke."

"Thanks." Keith sucked it down thirstily.

"You want one?" the same man asked Carl.

"I wouldn't mind." Before he could receive it, Carl shouted, "Charlotte! We're having a stiff one first!" As soon as he realized what he had said, the entire place broke up with laughter. Seeing Keith's smirk, Carl moaned, "Oh, Christ, where's the booze?"

"If you want something stiff, you came to the right place, Carl!" came Charlotte's snappy reply.

"Here, love." A man handed Carl a glass.

Detecting a slight accent, Carl met the man's eyes. He was absolutely gorgeous. The heat of excitement washed over Carl's skin. "Thanks." He shot it down quickly and handed the stunning man back the empty glass.

"Anytime, love. Anytime."

Carl had to stop ogling him. There were so many handsome men in the room he was going crazy.

"Can we get rolling, honey pies?" Charlotte asked loudly.

"Yes, Mother!" Carl opened the top button of his cotton shirt, boiling hot suddenly.

"Okay! Cue the music and lights!"

Loud dance music blasted and swirls of colored lights began spinning around them.

"How the hell are we supposed to say dialogue over this?" Keith waved to the surroundings.

"That's her fucking problem."

Over an amplified speaker, they heard, "Gay dance scene. Take one. Action!"

Carl had no idea what they should be doing. So he grabbed Keith by the hips and connected their crotches together, dancing cock to cock.

In response, Keith wrapped his arms around Carl's neck, licking his skin and chewing on his shirt collar.

Carl felt his body tingle and caught the eyes of the men as they surrounded them. Though they were trying to act normal, every one of them was keeping track of his and Keith's actions.

Feeling Keith step back, dancing with his arms over his head in sudden wild abandon, Carl blinked in awe. Someone behind Keith reached around him, pulling Keith's t-shirt over his head.

Carl had no idea what to do. Should they stop? Break the scene? Keith seemed to be loving it. The look on his face was pure bliss.

With his shirt off, and most likely gone for good, Keith began unbuttoning Carl's. As Carl held his breath, moving to the deep, throbbing beat, he felt the warm air brushing his naked skin.

Raising his head to see where the cameras were, Carl just noticed two nearly naked men, dancing erotically, touching their hard-ons through their g-strings and pulling their small garments down their hips, nearly exposing themselves.

"Holy shit," Carl mumbled, knowing no one could hear.

Keith removed Carl's shirt. They were dancing topless in the leering crowd. Keith wrapped around Carl, licking his chest and pumping his hips into Carl's.

A camera made an aggressive appearance, parting the crowd like the Red Sea. As Keith devoured the skin on Carl's chest, it closed in on the action. Suddenly Carl felt as if he needed to react, participate, when all he had been doing was observing the surroundings like a stunned spectator.

Noticing some men kissing, Carl held Keith's face and directed it toward his mouth. The minute they connected, Keith went wild. Carl closed his eyes, pretending they weren't being spied by so many men and several cameras, and deepened the kiss. Keith opened the top button on Carl's slacks and dug his hand into them. When Keith made contact with Carl's cock, Carl knew this was going too far. Gently he urged Keith's fingers back out on the pretext of holding his hand. In seconds Keith had pulled out of his grasp using both his palms to slide down Carl's back to cup his bare ass inside his slacks.

With Keith humping his crotch, causing arousing friction, Carl felt his cock go rigid. He wrapped his arm around Keith's waist and lifted him off the floor, sucking at his tongue, moaning in agony. They weren't here; they were alone in their bedroom. *Oh, God please let this be a dream*!

Carl needed to slow Keith down. He had no idea what had come over him.

~

Keith was so horny he was about to explode. He didn't know what was in that drink, but whatever it was, it made his cock rock hard. He wanted Carl naked. Squeezing his ass cheeks in his palms, Keith felt the firmness of Carl's perfect bottom and the hard bulge of Carl's cock against his. Their tongues dancing around each other, the thrill of all the gorgeous men surrounding them, and the perfect muscle-bound dancers, Keith had never felt so uninhibited and free. He wanted to strip, hop up on the stage, and dance buck-naked.

In his ear, Carl hissed, "Slow down."

Opening his eyes, Keith came face to face with a camera lens. For a moment, just a split second, Keith had lost himself in the fantasy. But this wasn't a dream, this was a taping.

He removed his hands from Carl's butt cheeks and wrapped them around his waist.

"Sorry," he breathed in reply. "I don't know what came over me." Keith felt slightly disoriented. "Don't we have lines? Dialogue?"

"How the hell are we supposed to say them in this noise?"

G.A. Hauser

"Shout?"

"Fine." Carl leaned back and met Keith's eyes.

"Are you enjoying yourself?" Carl struggled to be heard.

"Yes! I love it! I don't know why I was so apprehensive."

Keith waited for the next line as Carl seemed to be surveying the area. Looking for Charlotte? Keith imagined he was.

"I don't know why either, Dennis!" Carl announced, "We can be free to be ourselves."

Keith arched his back and rubbed his hard cock up and down Carl's, still dancing in the madness.

Carl jerked Keith back to his mouth to whisper, "What are you doing?"

"Dancing!"

Carl released him, moving in a more determined rhythmic dance apart from his lover's contact.

Watching enthralled, Keith ignited from the way Carl's muscled torso shimmered in the colorful lights. The men around them were salivating, as if they couldn't get enough.

～

Carl kept waiting for the scene to end. What the fuck else did Charlotte need? They danced, they kissed, they had spoken their dialogue. *Hello? Cut? Anyone want to say cut?*

Keith opened the button on his jeans and pulled down his zipper. Carl thought Keith had lost his mind. Reaching for him, connecting their hips, Carl hissed, "What the fuck are you doing?"

"I told you, dancing."

"Stop undressing!"

"It feels right."

"Keith!" Carl was about to end this scene himself. Why the hell was Charlotte waiting? Making a deliberate sweep of the room, Carl finally found her. She was kneeling up on the bar behind a camera, obviously watching them on the monitor.

It was impossible for Carl to catch her eye unless he broke character and began waving his arms like a lunatic.

Keith began tugging his pants down. Carl gripped them in his fingers, keeping them on Keith's hips. "You'll regret this if you do it."

"Let me have fun."

"Keith, she's filming it."

"I know."

"Stop it."

"Just down to my briefs."

"Keith!"

Keith shoved Carl back and lowered his jeans down his thighs. The men in the room went absolutely wild.

They egged Keith on, circling around the two of them, clapping and whistling. A nearly nude go-go boy hopped off the stage and made his way over.

As Carl watched in awe, Keith spun his jeans over his head and tossed them aside. The sight of Keith's huge bulge under his briefs was making Carl dizzy.

The gorgeous erotic dancer wrapped around Keith's waist and humped his body.

The noise level had reached a fevered pitch. When both their tiny garments began coming off, Carl pushed his way to Charlotte. Muscling through the madness, Carl shoved the camera lens away from filming. "Charlotte! Cut, for God's sake, cut! Charlotte!"

$\sim$

Keith was high. The sight of all the fantastic men in the room, their hungry leers, their sleek bodies, masculine scent, and deep voices, was making Keith so horny he had completely lost control. A fantastic nearly naked dancer was rubbing his enormous erection against his. Keith couldn't believe the charge of electricity flowing through his veins. He wanted to strip naked for these men to admire him, for them to jack off while staring at him. And he wanted one of them to suck him, or better yet, let him fuck Carl while everyone watched.

Through the insanity, someone grabbed Keith from behind, picking him up off his feet. He was carried off the dance floor by a strong man.

Once he was shoved into the men's room, he spun around to see Carl's fury.

"Shit." Keith swallowed in anguish.

"What the hell are you doing?" Carl yelled. "Are you insane? Don't you realize Charlotte is filming this?"

Keith touched his own face, backing up and hitting the tiled wall.

"Keith!" Carl rushed to catch him. "Are you all right?"

"I feel very light headed."

"You're acting like an exhibitionist! None of this is scripted, Keith."

"I know. I don't know what came over me." Keith staggered to the sink and splashed his face.

When someone came in, Carl spun around in anger.

Charlotte was standing in the room. "Is everything all right?"

"What the hell was in that fucking drink, Charlotte?" Carl asked.

"Drink?" She appeared shocked.

"Why don't you find Keith's clothes? Make yourself useful!" Carl snarled as she left.

Keith began to tremble. "Carl, I'm sorry."

"Don't worry about it. Come here." Carl reached out.

Keith fell against him, closing his eyes. The sense of security Carl represented to Keith made him feel so much better. He didn't want to let him go.

The door opened again and Charlotte held out Keith's jeans.

"Get dressed, Keith." Carl nudged him to stand on his own.

Shaking in anxiety, Keith took his pants and slipped them back on. "Please tell me you won't use any of that for the show, Charlotte."

"Keith, it was really hot."

"Charlotte!" Carl approached her, menacing.

"Did you see the reaction of those men? Oh, Keith, please. You have to let me at least use splices of it."

"Oh, Christ," Keith moaned, feeling like the worst fool.

Before Carl began another tirade, Charlotte moved to Keith's side, touching his shoulder. "Keith, sweetie, listen to me."

"What?" Keith knew exactly what she was going to say.

"Tiny snippets. I promise. Nothing more than thirty seconds. I swear, your character will soar to number one all time best drama characters. Think Emmys, think BANFF, the Nationals! Keith! This will catapult you into another class of actors."

"Carl?" Keith knew he wasn't thinking straight and he needed Carl's clear headed advice.

Carl stood next to him. "Charlotte, be honest with us, please."

"I am. Look, boys, you know my television series are always racy. But," she stopped them before they interrupted her, "which show won best cable drama 2007?"

"*The Ties That Bind*," Carl sighed.

Keith knew that was Charlotte's show.

"Who won best actor and actress?" she urged.

Looking at Carl, Keith met his eyes and asked, "Carl?"

"Her stars won, Keith," Carl admitted. "Both awards."

"Best direction? Most erotic scene, hottest nighttime soap?"

"You." Carl crossed his arms over his bare chest.

"Would I steer either of you wrong?"

"No." Carl looked down at his shoes.

"Keith?" she asked, imploring.

"Snippets?"

She rubbed her index finger on her thumb. "Itsy bitsy."

"All right."

Charlotte hugged him. "I adore both of you."

She kissed each of their cheeks, and said, "That's it. All done for today. Get a ride back to the studio and change. Pick up the new script before you go. See you tomorrow."

When she raced out of the room, Keith could feel the wind of her wake.

Carl reached out for Keith's hand. Keith took it and they made their way out of the men's room. A roar of applause erupted at their appearance.

Releasing their contact, Keith walked through the crowd of men in what felt like a standing ovation. Melvin handed them each their shirts, a knowing smirk on his face.

Some of the men patted his back, others reached out to shake Keith's hand. He imagined Carl behind him going through the same thing.

"Thanks, Keith." A young blond haired man held Keith's hand in a tight grip. "Your support means a lot to the gay community."

That puzzled Keith. Support? What on earth did he mean? All he was doing was playing a gay character. "Sure. No problem."

When they stepped outside, their car was waiting.

Keith tucked in his shirt and climbed into the back seat as the driver held the door. A scream of the fans that had collected at the barricade rang out at their presence.

Once he and Carl were closed inside the car, Keith looked over at him. Carl appeared very tired.

"I'm sorry, babe."

Carl pointed to the driver and shook his head for Keith to be quiet.

They arrived back at the studio and changed into their own clothing. An assistant there handed out the new scripts. They left in silence, walking through the parking lot to Carl's car.

Chapter Four

Once Carl had them moving down the road, he scolded, "What on earth were you thinking?"

"I'm sorry. I have no idea what came over me."

"Keith! On film? And you think that's going to help you stay in the closet?"

"Carl, honest, I was swept up in it. I couldn't believe how liberating it was. Men! Gay men! Dancing together, getting naughty. It was so amazing."

When Carl's hand grasped his, Keith turned to look at his face. "It was, Keith. It was amazing."

Exhaling in relief, Keith responded, "I was so horny I thought I was going to explode."

"That dancer was gorgeous. Did you see the size of the dick on him?"

"Christ! He was rubbing it on mine. I was dying."

"Some of the men in that room were extraordinary."

"I know." In excitement Keith pushed on his own crotch with his free hand.

"It's no wonder gay relationships don't last."

Keith sighed heavily. "So many willing men…who would have known?"

"It's like a secret society."

"It is, Carl. I feel the same way. We were going about our business, dating women, completely ignorant of this underground gay thing."

"Not so underground. That's a very big club."

"It was enormous. And the amount of men in it…holy cow. Can you imagine watching naked male dancers and drinking booze? I'd be fucking strangers every night."

"I know. It's crazy. I suppose the only way to have a committed relationship is to never expose yourself to that kind of easy sex."

"Yeah, but now we know it exists."

"And?" Carl pulled into the parking garage of his condo.

"And?" Keith released Carl's hand and held the script.

"Are you planning on going to gay nightclubs now and cheating on me?"

"No. Don't be ridiculous, Carl." Keith wanted Carl to come with him, so they could screw the same man together.

Carl parked in his garage and shut the engine. "God knows what's in store for us in the next episode."

As Keith exited the car, he mumbled, "Hope it's more gay disco."

"What?" Carl asked, using his remote to close the garage door.

"Nothing."

Coming through the lobby door, Keith noticed a photographer standing out in front of their building, having a smoke. He shoved Carl back out into the parking garage. "Is there a back way?"

"The stairs." Carl jogged across the concrete to the stairwell using his master key to get in. They climbed the long hike up six floors and rushed to get inside the condo.

Once they had, Keith kicked off his shoes and tossed the script down on the table. "Beer…I need a beer."

After Keith grabbed two and opened the tops, he searched for Carl. Carl was in the study, sitting at his computer. Placing Carl's beer in front of him, Keith waited for the computer to set up, sucking the ale down as he did. He already knew what Carl was going to look for. YouTube.

Going to Google, putting their names and YouTube into the search engine, they found the site instantly. Keith pushed Carl back to sit on his lap as they waited for it to download.

"Ready?" Carl asked.

"I suppose." Keith wrapped his arm around Carl's shoulder, taking a long draw of his beer as he gazed at the screen.

Music played loudly. Carl used the mouse to shut it off. A slightly fuzzy image of the two of them naked appeared. In the glowing reddish light, Keith knelt up naked, his dick erect and protruding away from his body, as Carl pretended to give him head.

"I'm not even in your mouth."

"Nope. You're not. But it's a good shot of your cock, babe."

Keith kept watching. He knew what came next because he remembered the shoot perfectly. Carl had him get to his hands and knees. And Carl's partially erect cock never penetrated his ass. It obviously was too low.

"I knew it. It's all so blatantly clear this is for the show." Carl picked up his beer.

"Sucks having our cocks on video," Keith sighed.

"At least it's our rehearsed love scene. Any moron can see we're not really doing it."

"Let me read the comments." Keith nudged Carl to move the cursor lower.

"It says, 'I love these guys. I hope just because they're a gay couple that people will leave them alone'." Carl breathed softly. "That's actually pretty nice."

"Look at that one." Keith pointed to the screen. "They get me so horny I masturbate to the television."

Carl laughed. "Whoa. Bad boy."

"All in all, not horrible." Keith stood off Carl's lap.

"No. Like I said, any moron can see it's all fake sex." Carl closed YouTube down and scanned the rest of the Google entries. "Look at how many fan sites there are, Keith."

Leaning down over Carl's shoulder, Keith watched as Carl flipped screens, their names and *Forever Young* on page after page.

As Carl entered a few sites to read the dirt, Keith left him to it, reclining on the sofa in the living room. He imagined going back to that club again, on their own, without a camera crew. Keith fantasized picking one fantastic stud out of the crowd and he and Carl devouring him together.

When he heard his mobile phone ringtone, he reached into his jeans' pocket. Checking the display, he sighed unhappily. "Hello, Mother."

"Keith. You never even told us you moved. That's not right, Keith."

"After the way Dad reacted to me having a gay television role? Are you joking?" He sat up and drank more of his beer.

"You moved in with Carl, didn't you?"

"Who told you?"

"Patty."

"Oh, nice!" Keith grew upset at his ex-roommate.

"We also read it in the tabloids, Keith. So don't take it out on her."

"Whatever." Keith balanced the beer on a coaster on the coffee table.

"Can we have his address?"

"Why? So Dad can come over and harass us?"

"He won't do that, Keith. Please. Your sister and I would like to know."

"How's Nadine doing? I haven't spoken to her in ages."

"She's fine. She was asking about you yesterday. She wants us all to get together."

"I can't. The schedule's too tight." He watched Carl come in the room. "Mom," he mouthed to him.

Carl nodded, setting his beer bottle in the sink.

"The tabloids say you and Carl are a couple."

"Of course they do. And you know how reliable they are. Remember Elvis giving birth to the alien? I swore by that one."

"All right, Keith, no need to be smart mouthed."

"We're friends. Okay? Friends."

"I believe you."

"Thank you." Keith unzipped his pants and pulled his cock out of his jeans so he could tease Carl when he turned to look.

"Are you dating a woman now?"

"I don't have time." When Carl glanced over, Keith flapped his cock at him. Carl made a face that Keith knew was wicked admonishment for him behaving like a sexual deviant.

"Suck it," Keith said silently.

"How is Patty getting along without you?"

"I suppose she's okay. I found her a roommate."

Carl crouched down next to him.

"Oh. That was nice of you."

"It was the least I could do." The heat of Carl's mouth surrounded his cock. Keith stifled a moan in pleasure.

"Your father won't watch the show anymore."

"I figured." Keith closed his eyes.

"He says it disgusts him."

"Yeah. Gay sex disgusts me too." Keith raised his hips, sinking deeper into Carl's mouth.

"I'm surprised to hear you say that after the argument you and your father had the last time we saw you."

"Oh, yeah. Gay fucking and sucking? Sick stuff." Keith pumped into Carl's tight mouth.

"You should tell that to your father. Maybe you two can make amends."

"Ah!" Keith bit his lip. "Yes. Well, you pass it on to him. Tell him there's nothing worse than a man sucking on your dick."

"Keith!"

"Sorry to be so crass. Gotta go. Bye, Mom." He hung up, dropped the phone on the carpet and groaned.

"You are so evil!" Carl laughed, squeezing Keith's cock in his hand.

"Keep sucking, you perverted cock-sucker."

"I love it when you talk dirty," Carl crooned.

Once Carl had resumed, Keith inched his own shirt up his chest. "You love when I talk dirty? Okay, how about this. You and me."

Carl moaned, sucking him down to the root.

"Going wild together, stripping each other naked…"

Carl dragged Keith's jeans lower on his hips, trying to get at his balls.

Keith felt his body begin to ascend to heaven. "And double fucking a go-go boy."

Carl choked and sat up, releasing Keith's cock from his lips. "What?"

"Oh, you stopped…" Keith pouted.

"A go-go boy? Come on, Keith. Now that you've had a gay club experience you're going to cheat on me?"

"Not cheat. Share him." Keith touched his own dick, feeling Carl's saliva on it.

"Share? And somehow you think that's going to be a good idea and not fuck up our relationship?" Carl stood, leaving the room.

"Carl!" Keith scrambled to go after him.

~

Carl stared at their bed trying to understand Keith's motivation. Yes, today was wild and crazy. He agreed the men in that club were beautiful, sexy, but…try to hide their sexuality while the paparazzi follow them to that renowned gay nightclub where men danced nude and gay men kissed? Yeah right!

"Carl…"

Looking over his shoulder, he found Keith with his shirt hiked up his chest and his pants at his thighs. His cock was rock hard and blushing in color. The act was so overt, Carl knew Keith wanted to take his clothing off for men. Other men.

Moving across the carpet to him, Carl touched Keith's protruding penis gently. "It gets you off, doesn't it?"

"I don't know why."

Carl removed Keith's shirt, tossing it on the bed. "Are you an exhibitionist?"

"I never thought I was."

Pushing Keith's jeans and briefs down, Carl stripped him of his lower clothing. "How hot does the idea make you?"

"Insane. It makes me insane."

"But you really struggled with the nude scenes on the set. You almost passed out when you found out we were naked on YouTube."

"I did. But that's different. I don't want my sex with you to be in the public domain. But that shouldn't affect what we can do in private. With no cameras."

"Oh? Private? Like at a gay club private? Keith you're not making sense. Do you like the idea of exposing yourself to other men or not?" Carl smoothed his fingers along the length of Keith's cock. It was so hard it felt like stone.

"Yes. It's not the same surrounded by gay men. And to be honest, Carl, the thought of that YouTube video was worse than the reality. I think what upsets me is our private lovemaking being exposed." Keith's chest began rising and falling rapidly.

"Oh? Suddenly the man who was straight two months ago, living with and making love to a woman, wants to have a threesome with a go-go dancer?"

"Yes…" Keith hissed, trusting his hips against Carl's hand.

"I don't get it."

"Neither do I." Keith wrapped his arms around Carl's neck, pumping his cock in and out of Carl's palm.

"And if I say no, I don't like the idea, you'll start cheating on me? Sneaking around?"

"Never. It's either with you, or nothing."

"But," Carl felt slightly let down for so many reasons, "you just said last night that maybe we don't need rubbers…you know, between you and me."

"I did say that."

"If we start playing around with strange men…"

"We'd be safe."

"I know we'd be safe, but I'd want us to continue using rubbers between us."

"Why?"

"Because. Keith, you're talking about bringing the unknown into our clean union."

Shaking his head, Keith replied, "You're right. No. It's insane. I don't know why I was thinking that. Forget it. I'd rather have sex with you without condoms, than have sex with others and need them."

"Have you ever been tested?"

"No. You?"

"No. I guess since I've always used rubbers with the women I've had, I never imagined I'd need one."

"Me too. I've never had unprotected sex."

Carl stopped stroking Keith's cock and urged him to lie next to him in the bed. Relaxing, clothed, while Keith was nude, Carl touched Keith's shoulder, running his hand down his arm to his fingers. "How many women have you had sex with?"

"Two."

"Two?" Carl was surprised. "Patty and one other person?"

"Yes. My girlfriend in high-school, Annette."

"Really? What the hell did you do in college? You were celibate?"

"Yes. I was really into my acting classes. I spent all my time volunteering for extra credit. Honest. I didn't have a girlfriend in college. What about you? How many women did you sleep with?"

"I've had around ten I think."

"Ten? Ten girlfriends or ten fucks?"

"Ten girlfriends. Ten fucks?" Carl rolled his eyes at the absurdity.

"Then you're the whore not me."

"I suppose I am." Carl smiled. "But I've never had sex without a rubber. Never."

"You ever get anything? Any bugs?"

"No. I've been lucky. I'm completely clean."

"Me too."

"Do you want me to get an AIDS test before we do it unprotected?"

Keith stared at him for a long moment.

"Keith? I will. I don't mind."

"No. If you've never had sex without a rubber, I suppose there's no need."

Carl cupped his jaw. "You sure?"

"When was the last time you slept with a woman?"

"I think I mentioned it to you. There was a woman who worked on the set. We did it twice. But that was almost a year ago now."

"You never touched a boy? Never? Not even in school?'

Knowing he had, Carl smiled sweetly. "I did jerk another guy off in college. We were stoned off our asses at a Rolling Stones concert."

Keith cracked up.

"Yeah, well, what can you do?" Carl grinned wryly.

"I never did anything like that."

"I suppose that's why I find it inconceivable that you want to go a little man crazy."

Keith became shy and lowered his eyelashes.

It gave Carl a moment to drink in his naked body. Keith's cock had settled down and hung limply over his large sack. Carl thought Keith was absolutely perfect. His skin was bronze and smooth, right down to where a Speedo would hug his hips. "You're such a pin-up boy."

Keith's eyes immediately met Carl's.

Drawing nearer on the bed, Carl ran his hand over Keith's rough jaw and into his blond hair. Bringing him to his lips, Carl kissed him, licking at the tip of Keith's tongue, toying with it inside his mouth.

That lovely whimper emerged from Keith that Carl loved so much. Urging him to lie on his back, Carl smoothed his hand down Keith's chest and bumped into his erection. Grabbing it and fisting it a few times, Carl wanted to please his lover, and if that meant experimenting with another man, was that okay?

It was something Carl would have to think long and hard over. Long and hard. Smiling to himself, that was exactly how he would describe Keith's dick.

~

Keith splayed out on the bed as Carl stroked him. He was asking too much. He knew that. In reality he didn't need anything more than Carl. Carl fulfilled him in every way. This craving to play dirty was just a fantasy. They would never act on it.

Bending his knees and holding one in each hand, Keith crooned, "Fuck me."

Instantly responding, Carl stood off the bed and undressed, setting the lube and condoms out.

Before Carl prepared them, he nestled between Keith's spread legs.

Feeling Carl's light flickering tongue on his ass, Keith felt his dick bob and go rock hard. "Jesus, Carl…"

Carl had never done that to him before. It seemed each time they made love they discovered something new and exciting. Keith was convinced this was all he needed. It was perfect.

As Carl's tongue became bolder, licking more aggressively, Keith grabbed his own cock and jerked it a few times. Carl moved to suck on his balls, drawing them into his mouth one at a time. Keith released his cock because he knew he would come and he wanted to wait, to make it last, to come while Carl was inside him.

After a tantalizing amount of lapping and sucking on his testicles, Carl moved higher, teasing Keith's erection with the tip of his tongue. "Carl…you are amazing."

Once Carl had plunged Keith's cock into his mouth all the way to the base a few times, he sat up and reached for the condoms.

"No." Keith stopped him. "Just lube."

"You sure?"

"Yes. I want to feel your skin." They'd had the "safe sex" lesson pounded into them all their lives. But he trusted he and Carl were clean.

Carl tossed the condoms aside. He squeezed the tube of gel into his hand and massaged Keith's ass with it.

The surge to his loins at the penetration almost made Keith shoot his load. Biting back the urge, wanting to come with Carl inside him, Keith closed his eyes and had to stop gazing at Carl. The man was so damn fantastic, staring at him naked was enough to make Keith climax. When Carl's fingers drew away, Keith opened his eyes. Watching Carl smooth glistening liquid on his cock was easily as arousing as dancing with a well-hung go-go boy.

Carl pushed Keith's knees back to expose his ass better. As Keith licked his lips in anticipation, Carl's unsheathed penis slid effortlessly inside him.

"Aaah…" Carl was obviously enjoying the sensation.

"Good?" Keith felt a shiver of pleasure rush through him, even more so at his lover's reaction.

"Oh, yes..." Carl pushed in to the hilt.

Keith relished the sensation of being filled by him. There was nothing better than giving everything to the man you adored. "Carl...so nice."

"Christ, it does feel better without."

"I knew it would." Keith touched his own cock, feeling it seep, rubbing the sticky drip around the head.

Carl began thrusting, long, slow, and deep. Watching Carl's face as he began the climb to heaven, Keith kept slowly stroking on his own cock, but wanted to wait. Now he wanted to fuck Carl.

Biting his lip, Keith felt the urge to come so badly he had to stop touching himself. Gripping the bed under him, he gazed in awe as Carl's hips quickened their pace and his balls began slapping Keith's bottom.

The second before Carl came, he opened his green eyes. The breath caught in Keith's throat as he met that stare. Just as Carl's cock shivered inside him, Carl grunted a deep, animalistic sound and squeezed out, "I love you!" with it.

"Holy shit, Carl..." Keith admired him as Carl caught his breath, the dewy sweat of sex covering Carl's body. "You gorgeous mother fucker."

A weary chuckle escaped Carl as he recuperated.

After one last thrust in, Carl pulled out. "Keith. That is fantastic."

"I intend to find out for myself."

"Let me wash up. Hang on."

"I'm hanging." Keith couldn't stop staring at Carl as he climbed off the bed stiffly and staggered to the bathroom.

Pulling on his cock as he waited, Keith had an image flash of that club. The men. The nudity.

Carl returned, standing near the bed. "Ready, babe."

Keith moved over, allowing Carl to lie on his back. As he

knelt between Carl's legs, Keith felt the trickle of Carl's sperm running down his thigh, and loved it. As the rush of excitement washed over him, Keith dove between Carl's legs and exposed his ass, licking Carl the way Carl had licked him, but much more aggressively.

I am getting into this so much!

Keith pressed his hips into the sheets under him, squirming on the mattress, so hot to come he was burning up.

Unable to tolerate the wait any longer, Keith sat up and reached for the lubrication. Kneeling between Carl's thighs, Keith used two fingers and entered inside Carl's body.

Instantly Carl hissed out a breath of air and his hips elevated off the mattress.

Keith stroked his prostate until Carl was rock hard again and shivering with pleasure. Coating his own cock, Keith was so excited he knew just pushing inside Carl without a condom would tip him over the edge. Keith had never had sex without one. He had no idea how much different it would feel.

When he slid in, skin on skin, Keith felt a passionate rush that was indescribable. There was so much more sensation, it was truly a tactile experience. "Carl!"

"I know."

"Holy shit...oh, this is amazing." Keith deepened his penetration. When he couldn't push in any farther, he held still, delighting in their union. "Sex with you is so spiritual."

He heard Carl stifle a chuckle.

"I mean it, Carl. It's the way we show each other how much we love each other."

"I know, Keith."

"If I move, I'll spurt." Keith could feel his cock pulsating in the tight heat.

"Spurt for me, lover."

Pulling out to the tip, Keith dove back in again deeply. Repeating it, slowly gliding in and out as far as he could go without falling out, Keith continued the tantalizing action until he couldn't stand it anymore.

Deciding now was the time, Keith upped his tempo. He drove his cock in and out rapidly, feeling the pleasure begin deep inside his balls. Opening his mouth for air, closing his eyes tightly, Keith had another flash of fucking in front of all those men in the club and ejaculated so hard he felt as if he were having a fit.

His hips jerked forward until he was inside Carl so deeply he felt like his balls were being fucked as well. A strangled moan squeezed out of his throat as his entire body clenched.

"Holy Christ, Keith!" Carl breathed as if he were in awe watching him.

As the sensation subsided, Keith braced himself on the bed, hanging his head and gasping for air.

Keith looked down at the sight of his slick penis inside his lover's ass. It was so beautiful it brought the tears to his eyes. "Carl…"

"Aw…come here, baby."

Staring at the connection as he pulled out as slowly as he could, Keith bit his lip on an emotional outburst of love and adoration. "I…I have to wash up."

When they disconnected, Carl moved closer to hug him. "I love you."

Choking in a sob, Keith replied, "I love you too, Carl."

"Let me help."

Carl assisted Keith, getting him to his feet.

With more love and devotion than even his own mother had shown him as a child, Carl lovingly washed Keith's body.

The soapy washcloth ran along his still rock hard cock. Keith gazed at the action with blurry eyes. His bottom was cleansed, his anatomy tended and dried, Keith waited for Carl to wipe his own body clean before he reacted. Once Carl tossed the washcloth aside, Keith grabbed him, crushing him in his embrace. "Don't ever leave me. No matter what."

"Promise, my beautiful lover. I promise."

Chapter Five

"Hello?" Keith answered his cell phone. He and Carl were in the middle of memorizing their new dialogue.

"Keith O'Leary?"

"Yes?"

"Jeff Palmer. Adam Lewis told me you were looking for a publicist."

Keith sat up and whispered to Carl, "Publicist."

Acknowledging him, Carl sat down on the sofa next to Keith, tossing the script on the coffee table.

"Yes. Did he give you any information about me?"

"He said you were gay and looking to hide it."

That shocked Keith. "Holy shit."

"Don't worry. It's not unusual. You just let me handle it for you."

"Could you do the same for Carl Bronson?"

"He's the star you're living with, right?"

"Yes."

"Let me tell you first off, living together was a mistake."

Crushed by the comment, Keith reached for Carl's hand.

"But, saying that, meeting in secret and going to each others' homes isn't much better."

"What do you suggest?"

"Women. Plain and simple, Keith. You and Carl have got to be seen in public with women."

"Do you arrange that?"

"I do. That's what you pay me for."

"Okay. Tell me what to do." Keith met Carl's eyes as they riveted to his.

"I'll set you both up with some girlfriends. We have our own photographers planted with the paparazzi to sell their photos to the tabloids. We get you two shot with the women and start spreading the gossip that you're both involved. Any award ceremony, they show up. You got it?"

"Got it." Keith felt so sick to his stomach he was in pain.

"And you two, don't even think about holding hands or kissing in public. That's a very big no-no."

"Okay." Keith wondered if Carl could hear him. The voice over the line was very loud.

"No gay affiliation."

"What does that mean?" Keith began taking offense.

"Don't hang out in public with other known gay men. No gay bars, no gay film festivals—"

"Hang on a minute…" Keith released Carl's hand so he could clench his fist. "Let's not forget the characters we play are gay and we support freedom of choice."

Dead silence fell on the other line.

"Mr. Palmer?" Keith wondered if he hung up.

"You want to remain in the closet? Is that the idea?"

Keith turned to face Carl as Carl caressed the nape of his neck affectionately.

"Yes, but—"

"Keith, listen to me." The man inhaled a deep breath. "You and Carl Bronson have got to wash your hands of that idea. You got it? You go to ballgames, car races, be seen watching beauty pageants, and no…I repeat, no gay affiliations. Is that clear?"

"That sucks!" Keith didn't want to become some silent partner in gay pride.

"That's reality. Do you want to come out?"

"I fucking want to! But Adam says that my career would be over."

"Calm down, Keith."

Keith took a deep breath. "I'm sorry I swore."

Carl hugged Keith tight in support.

"It isn't anything I haven't heard before. Now, I told you what you have to do to keep the tabloid bastards off your back. The question is, do you want me to do it?"

Dabbing at a threatening tear, Keith grabbed Carl and held on for dear life. "Yes."

"Okay. I'll set up the date with the women. It's got to be soon, Keith. The rags are after you two with a vengeance."

"I know."

"This Friday. I'll call with a time and send a car to pick you both up. It'll be leaked to the press and the paparazzi. You will be seen with these women. Act like you are attracted to them. For pity's sake, Keith, you and Carl have got to hold their hands. Act! It's what you two do best, right?"

Keith wanted to tell Mr. Jeff Palmer what he and Carl really did best, but refrained. "Fine."

"Good."

"Where do you get these women from? Are they trustworthy?"

"They work for me. Yes. Don't worry about that."

"It's all so damn sickening."

"I don't make the rules, kid."

"I know. Thanks, Mr. Palmer. I suppose this is what we need to do to survive."

"Write my number down in case you need me or have any questions."

Keith whispered to Carl. "Pen and paper?"

Carl jumped up, quickly returning with it.

"Go ahead, Mr. Palmer." Keith wrote his number down.

"You'll hear from my office in a couple of days."

"Okay." Keith disconnected the call and tossed the phone on the table. He gave Carl a pained look. "This sucks."

"I heard most of it. The guy talks very loudly."

"Then you should be feeling as sick as I do right now."

"Keith," Carl held both Keith's hands, "I know you would you rather we came out as a couple. Okay? I know."

"We can't. I understand that. If we do, this series will be our last. Carl, I'm only twenty-six. I can't stop acting after this one hit show."

"Then we have to pretend, Keith. There's no other choice."

Covering his face with his hands as the anger filled him, Keith felt Carl's warm cuddle. "That means your fantasy of a three-way with a go-go boy is out."

"Just shoot me."

"At least he didn't order us to move apart."

Lowering his hands, Keith met Carl's loving green eyes. "No. We at least have that."

"That's a lot."

"It is." Keith kissed him.

"Let's finish working. I feel like I almost have the lines memorized."

"Oh, Carl," Keith groaned, wrapping his arms around Carl's neck.

"It's okay, babe. Whatever we need to do, we'll do it."

Closing his eyes, Keith inhaled Carl's wonderful scent and sighed.

Chapter Six

A phone call alerted them that the car was downstairs. Carl hung up and buttoned his suit jacket. "You ready for this charade?"

"Fuck no. I can't stand the idea of wasting an evening with two mannequins when I'd rather be here butt-fucking you."

"It's only a few hours. Come on." Carl opened the front door and locked it behind them. Taking the elevator down, they immediately noticed a group of photographers out front of their condo complex. Carl inhaled deeply for courage and pushed open the door.

The cameras flashed and shouting began instantly. Tuning it out, Carl made for the black limousine and the chauffeur holding open the door.

They climbed into the back seat and closed out the horrible noise and flashing lights.

In silence they drove to another location. More photographers were waiting. Two pencil thin women in short dresses made their way to their car. Carl rubbed his hands together nervously.

The door was opened and they climbed into the back seat with Carl and Keith.

"Hey," the blonde greeted them. "I'm Holly Lacey, and this is Jade Winslow."

"Hi." Carl waved awkwardly.

"Who's with whom?" Keith smirked.

"They wanted me to be with Carl." Holly pointed to him.

"How quaint," Keith sneered, "two matching sets of blonds paired with brunettes."

"You two don't mind doing this?" Carl asked.

"It's our job," Jade whispered.

"Man, you two are cute!" Holly giggled. "Better in person."

"Thanks." Carl couldn't imagine this getting any more awkward or embarrassing.

"What do you two do when you're not pretending to be someone's girlfriends?" Keith obviously couldn't wipe the sour expression off his face.

"Model. We both model." Holly pulled her short dress down her thighs.

The car parked in front of the most conspicuous restaurant in Beverly Hills. This was where you go to be seen by everyone who is anyone. Spago's.

Obviously Mr. Palmer had done his job because the amount of paparazzi waiting out front was frightening. The chauffeur opened the back door and Carl climbed out, reaching his hand for Holly, who took it and exited the car gracefully. Behind him Keith escorted Jade.

The cameras clicked and hummed, people shouted their names, and Carl felt nauseated by the charade. *That's life in the fast lane.* Somewhere deep in his heart he felt like he was betraying not only himself and Keith but all his gay fans.

Picturing the supportive men at the club where they had filmed, guilt crept into Carl's mid-section. What a kick in the teeth this would be for them. Or would they understand it meant survival for them in the acting business? Carl had no idea.

They were fawned over, their names shouted out so loudly Carl wanted to crawl under a table and hide. It was the worst case of bad performing he'd seen in his life. Who exactly were they fooling with this pantomime?

Waiting politely as the women sat down, Carl and Keith

ended up across from each other, and instantly the urge to play with Keith under the table made Carl crazy.

"Thank you," Carl replied as he took a menu.

"Anything to drink?" the waiter asked.

"Wine?" Carl needed a shot of bourbon but knew this was a "play act" for the public and he needed to look content.

They all agreed and he ordered a bottle of red.

Everyone in the vicinity was staring and whispering. Carl imagined them quibbling, "Aren't they gay? What on earth are they doing with women?"

The waiter presented an obscenely expensive bottle of Chianti. Carl was so nervous he had no idea if he could eat. Their glasses were filled and they were left to scan the menu. Holly leaned over to bat her lashes at Carl. In the midst of this madness Carl was expected to act straight. It was almost more than he was willing to bear. In reality, all he wanted to do was share a quiet dinner with Keith, flirt, sexually tease each other to death, and go home and hump 'til they dropped.

As Holly whispered seductively, reaching out to hold his hand, Carl wondered why he didn't feel any attraction for her at all. He had dated women. He'd even screwed them. The realization that ever since he had tasted male flesh he was hooked was something Carl had not considered. But it was fact. Though Holly and her equally anorexic friend, Jade, were pretty models, they did nothing to stir the excitement in his crotch. Absolutely nothing.

~

Keith was grinding his jaw, borderline enraged. This travesty, this imitation of being heterosexual for the media was gnawing at his nerves. Jade wasn't even the type of woman he would have been attracted to pre-Carl. She was obviously shallow and self-absorbed. Most likely she'd never even allowed a slice of pizza into her mouth, let alone a man's cock. The thought of being paired up with her was slightly repulsive. Why? If Keith had met her while he was in college, wouldn't he have been thrilled to kiss her? Imagined screwing her?

Not now. Keith had a sample of what gay love was like. Felt the carnal craving that only men have for sex. Constant humping, thrusting, *get me into a hole* sex. How could anything compare to the intensity he and Carl shared in the bedroom? It was ludicrous to even imagine it. Having this brunette pucker her lips and play kissy-kissy with him made his cock deflate to the point of feeling impotent. He knew no matter what this woman did to him, she could never get a rise out of him.

As Jade touched him, tried to pretend and give the performance she was paid to do, Keith stared at Carl as he gazed back at him. It was murder. "Carl…" Keith hissed quietly.

Carl's eyes filled with tears. He twisted away to avoid looking at Keith.

"What will you have, honey?" Jade leaned on Keith's shoulder.

"What do you recommend?" Keith knew if he and Carl kept staring at each other, they would end up crying.

Jade pointed to a few meaningless suggestions. Keith wanted a hamburger or a pepperoni pizza. He didn't have the pallet for this extravagance. And who the hell was paying for it? Adam Lewis? Mr. Jeff Palmer? He sure as hell couldn't afford it. Obviously his paycheck would have some numbers skimmed off the top before it trickled its way into his bank account.

The waiter finally made his way over. Keith just wanted to get this absurd dinner over with. Waiting as their dates requested rabbit food, Keith ordered the halibut simply because it was the only item of food he noticed when he glanced at the selection.

Carl ordered the same and Keith knew he'd never even looked at the menu.

As their dates cuddled them, giggled, and kissed their cheeks, Keith caught Carl's gaze again. Silently, Keith mouthed, "I can't do this, Carl."

Carl dabbed at his eyes and whispered, "I have to go to the men's room. Will you excuse me?"

As Keith watched him go, he felt sick he couldn't run after him. Everyone was witnessing this performance. It had to be worth the time and expense. They had to play the dirty little game.

~

Carl pushed through the door and checked the room. One man was standing at the sink. Avoiding him, Carl entered a stall and leaned back against the door. The urge to sob was overwhelming. He couldn't do this. Biting back his anguish, Carl fought with himself to straighten up. He couldn't fall apart on their first public appearance with their "girlfriends". Even though he knew Keith did not want it, Carl hated seeing Jade touch him. Carl wanted to touch him. He wanted to be the one to smooth his hand across Keith's back, lean against his shoulder to whisper and flirt.

It had only been a few minutes and Carl was already spent. This farce was wearing heavily on him. There had to be another way.

"Carl?"

Hearing Keith's soft voice, Carl faltered, "Go away."

"I can't."

"You'll make the whole charade meaningless." Carl struggled with his emotions. "Go back to the table."

"Are you okay?"

"I will be. Give me a second."

The door rattled. "Carl, open this up."

Terrified someone would hear their conversation, Carl

opened the door to the stall and looked around. The room was vacant at the moment. "Keith, please go back and sit down."

"Carl..." Keith caressed his hair affectionately. "You're upset. I can't stand seeing you this way."

"I'm worse with your attention. Please. Go back and I'll just suck down the wine until I'm numb. Okay?"

Punching his fist against the metal stall frame, Keith snarled, "This bites!"

"Go!"

As if he were heading to his execution, Keith dragged his feet out of the bathroom.

Inhaling to gain some control, Carl moved to the sink and looked at his face. "This is not going to work. It's killing us."

~

"Everything okay?" Jade whispered, wrapping her arm around Keith's back after he sat down again.

"What do you think?" he scoffed.

"Hang in there." She hugged him and instantly returned to her adoring act.

The minute Carl returned, Keith watched him like a hawk. Carl looked ill.

"Welcome back, honey." Holly threw Carl kisses.

A weak smile was her reply.

The meal was placed in front of them. Keith had to force it down. The women fell into a conversation, barely eating a leaf of lettuce.

Both he and Carl had finished the wine and Keith craved more. But the price of a bottle of alcohol was nearing on insanity.

Christ, will this date ever end?

Keith threw his napkin on the table, lapped at the last drop of wine from his glass, and waved at the waiter. "Check please?"

"It has been taken care of, sir."

"Oh." Keith glanced at Carl. He met his eyes briefly but didn't reply.

Carl threw some cash down for a tip and made a move to end this horrible fiasco.

Hooked arm in arm with their dates, Keith followed Carl outside. The moment they hit the fresh evening air, the paparazzi went nuts, taking pictures. The women used the opportunity to pose for the occasion. Carl's forced smile looked more like a grimace to Keith. Jade kissed his cheek long enough to get it on film, as did Holly to a pouting Carl.

The women waved at the cameras with pasted smiles on their lips.

Carl and Keith stood by as the women climbed into the back seat, joining them. The door was closed and the car moved on.

Jade held Keith's hand. "I'm so sorry."

"It's not your fault." Keith looked back at the driver, but assumed he was under the employ of Jeff Palmer as well.

"It's not fair to you guys." Holly cuddled against Carl gently.

Keith inspected his lover. Carl appeared devastated. He wasn't saying anything.

They pulled in front of the girls' high-rise building. When the door opened they gave the men's cheeks a long smooch and made sure the waiting paparazzi cameras caught it. Waving, throwing kisses, they made their way inside their condominium.

The door closed and the car moved on.

Needing to erase this horrible night, Keith leaned over the front seat. "Go to Santa Monica Boulevard."

"Keith," Carl admonished.

"Shut up." Keith turned back to the driver. "Go to Phobar's, please. Park around the block and be on call."

"Keith!"

"Carl, shut up!"

The driver handed Keith his business card. "This has my cell phone number on it. Call me when you want me to come to the main entrance."

"Cool." Keith stuffed it into his jacket. "How much cash do you have, Carl?"

Carl checked his wallet.

As he opened it, Keith leaned in to look. "Give me that fifty." Keith took it and set it on the front seat next to the driver.

"Keith…" Carl moaned.

"Will you be quiet?"

"You realize if we do this, then the whole charade we just endured will be for nothing."

"Not necessarily. They got photos of us kissing women. No one has any idea we're going to the club."

"Except the hundred gay and bi guys inside."

Keith shrugged. "Any leak that comes out of there we can say was from the filming."

"Don't get naked."

"Aw, come on," Keith teased.

"Keith!"

"I won't! But I will play dirty with you."

"Are you planning on inviting someone back to our place?"

Keith's heart skipped a beat. "Can I?"

Carl buried his face in his hands.

Moving to Carl's side of the back seat, Keith nestled against him. "What if we leave it up in the air? See if we find some unbelievable stud we just have to have?"

"He'd sell his story to the tabloids, Keith."

"His word against ours."

"You know this is flirting with disaster."

The car stopped. Keith looked out the window. "Come on."

A slight smile turned the edges up Carl's mouth.

Pumping his fist in glee, Keith addressed the driver, "We'll be gone an hour to two hours, tops."

"Don't worry about it." He smiled sweetly.

Keith just noticed how handsome the chauffeur was. As they climbed out of the car, he whispered to Carl. "The driver's adorable."

"Is he?"

"Yes. And he's on Palmer's payroll."

"I didn't get a good look at him."

"Come on. Time to get revved up."

~

Carl was so paranoid someone would be filming this entrance into a notorious gay club he actually hid his face. Rubbing both hands over his cheeks, Carl didn't lower his arms until they were inside and met the bouncer for their cover charge. The minute the burly man recognized them, a big smile brightened his tough countenance.

"Hey!" he gushed. "No charge! Welcome, boys."

Keith was beaming. Just the look on his lover's face told Carl he had recovered from the earlier dinner disaster.

"Thanks." Carl reached out to shake the man's hand.

"No problem, man. Have fun."

Carl passed through the doorway and could hear the music, feeling it vibrating through his chest. The room didn't have the same calm fabricated atmosphere as it did during the filming. This was live gay nightlife. No script, no performances, just reality.

"Come on!" Keith grabbed Carl's hand and hurried his pace into the madness.

As they passed through the tight crowd they were noticed. One by one the men in the room began to recognize them and stare, gossip, or nudge their fellow man.

While Keith made a beeline to the bar, Carl caught the sight of flesh. Naked men were dancing erotically, fondling their huge erections as they did. Monitors played triple-x gay porn. The amount of male pheromones floating around the air was overwhelming. Carl began to get hard just witnessing the decadence.

Staying close to Keith out of insecurity as well as their emotional attachment, Carl was handed a mixed drink while Keith waited for his own. Sipping it, looking at the naked men dancing, Carl shook his head in awe.

A glass in his hand, Keith leaned against Carl's side and said, "I love it!"

"I'm shocked you do." Carl shouted in his ear in the noise.

"How can you not? Carl, it's amazing."

A gorgeous, sleek man approached them. Carl's breath caught in his throat at how sexy he was. He stood boldly before them and asked, "Aren't you Dennis and Troy from *Forever Young?*"

Before Carl could deny it, Keith advised the man, "We are."

"I love that show." The man grinned wickedly. "You two are hot."

As Keith lapped up the compliment, the man asked, "Are you out?"

"No!" Carl admitted, suddenly feeling foolish since they were inside a gay bar.

The man swept his gaze at the group of men surrounding them. They all seemed to be staring in their direction at the moment. As if to reassure him, the handsome man said, "Don't worry about it. Just have fun."

"I intend to." Keith's eyes were wild as he gulped his drink.

When the man vanished into the crowd, Keith downed his entire rum and Coke and grabbed Carl. "Dance with me."

Carl hurried to consume his booze, reaching past men's shoulders to place the glass on the bar. With Keith's hand clamped to his, Carl was dragged onto the floor. Rainbows of colored light shimmered over the horde of writhing bodies. Instantly transformed back to the dance scene from the taping,

Carl warmed up quickly and wished Melvin was there to hand off his sport jacket.

Keith was just as overheated. He removed his, reached for Carl's, and disappeared as he found a place to leave them. Dancing on his own momentarily, Carl lost himself on the two appealing naked men doing very naughty things to themselves while others watched and drooled. When Keith returned he was shirtless. Carl's cock reacted more to his lover's naked torso than to the go-go boys' huge erections.

Keith wrapped his arms around Carl's neck, their pelvises meeting and grinding together as they moved.

Having Keith, knowing this man was his, Carl suddenly felt so much pride and contentment he cupped the back of Keith's head and drew him to his lips. When Keith's tongue entered his mouth, Carl's body rocked with an explosion of passion. Snaking his hands around Keith's naked back, tightening their embrace, Carl forgot the rest of the room and focused on Keith's mouth.

~

Keith was in heaven. After two hours of excruciating fake dates, he felt much more relaxed. Here they could be themselves. The deep bass rumbled through his bones as Carl's bulging crotch pressed excitedly into his.

While they danced, Keith began to release Carl's shirt from his slacks. Once the tail was out, Keith ran his hands under the cotton material and up Carl's warm sides. The kissing grew hotter. Obviously Carl was going as crazy as Keith was. One by one, Keith opened the buttons of Carl's top. After it was undone, Keith spread it wide over Carl's ripped chest, lowering it down his arms.

Their mouths unwilling to disconnect, Keith rubbed his palms over Carl's erect nipples as Carl's tongue drove him insane. It slipped in and out of Keith's mouth, fucking him in an imitation of the craving to do it with his dick.

Keith managed to get Carl's shirt off, and tucked it into the back of his own slacks to get out of the way.

Their torsos naked and beginning to sweat, Keith sealed them together, tightening his embrace. Needing to breathe deeply to recover from the hot kissing, Keith rested his chin on Carl's shoulder and looked around. The smiles of the men who watched them made Keith feel warm and accepted. Like they belonged.

Swaying gently with Carl, inhaling his cologne, Keith's vision paused on the naked dancing men. One dancer met his eye, grinning wickedly as he fingered his long shaft. Keith licked his lips at the sight. As Carl rotated them slowly, Keith was able to take in a panoramic view of the room. The television monitor was playing gay porn. He had never watched porn movies in his life. Fascinated by this alternative career in the film industry, Keith held Carl for a moment to prevent him spinning him away from the set. Carl parted from Keith just enough to catch his eyes.

When Carl realized what Keith was staring at, he too paused to watch.

"My God," Keith hissed in Carl's ear.

"Wow." Carl replied, riveted to the action.

Keith suddenly thought the man on the film appeared familiar. He took another good look at the go-go boy. "Carl."

Carl leaned down so he could hear him.

"That naked dancer is one of the porn stars."

Straightening up, Carl stared at one image, then the other.

The same man in the room, playing with himself for the fans was simultaneously being broadcast taking it up the ass. That reality floored Keith.

Carl wrapped around Keith and kissed him, lifting Keith off the ground as he arched backwards.

Keith held on for dear life knowing the scenes of anal sex had most certainly stimulated Carl. In Keith's ear, Carl breathed hoarsely, "I have to fuck you. Let's go home."

Grabbing Carl's head in both hands, Keith planted a wet tongue kiss on his lips and moaned in agreement. While they were attached at the mouth, Carl began moving them out of the crowd.

Keith paused to catch his breath, raced to recover their jackets and his shirt, handing Carl his clothing.

Standing near the exit, they dressed, not bothering to button their shirts, covering up with their jackets. Keith held his mobile phone, dialing as Carl stroked Keith's ass hungrily. "Hey. Pick us up."

"You got it. Be there in one."

Pocketing the phone, Keith leapt onto Carl, wrapping his legs around Carl's hips, eating at his mouth and tongue.

The bouncer whispered, "Your car is out front."

Parting from the kiss, hopping to the floor, Keith winked at the burly man and held Carl's hand. When they hit the cool night air, they released contact with each other and sprinted to the waiting car. Diving into the back seat, Keith shoved Carl down under him, grinding on his hips and sucking at his face.

"I love you!" Keith panted, so hot he was about to combust.

"I love you too, babe." Carl ran his hands over Keith's bare chest as his shirt and jacket parted.

Spinning to look at the driver, Keith caught his dark eyes in the rear view mirror as he drove.

Keith lowered to Carl's ear to whisper, "Let's invite him in."

"Yeah? How good looking is he?"

"See for yourself." Keith rolled off Carl to allow him to sit up.

Carl ran his hand through his hair to tame it, asking the man something benign to get a look at him. "You, uh, have you been a driver for long?"

Keith covered his smile. He thought Carl was so damn cute.

"About a year."

"Do...do you work for Jeff Palmer?"

"I do."

Keith moved to an upright position on the bench seat so he could see the driver's eyes in the mirror. He was so excited at the potential of a wild three-way his cock was throbbing with his pulse.

"Have you ever modeled?" Carl asked softly.

"Yes. I have."

Keith caught Carl's quick glance. Carl gestured with his hands trying to communicate, "What next?"

Moving closer to their conversation, Keith blurted out, "Interested in some group sex?"

"Keith!" Carl choked at the impropriety.

"With you two?" the man asked.

"Yes," Keith replied.

"Fuck yeah!"

Smiling at Carl in satisfaction, Keith reached out for Carl's face. "Thank you. You are amazing."

"Anything for you, babe." Carl smiled dreamily at him.

~

The driver stopped at the front entrance. Carl was so relieved to see it empty of vultures he actually thanked God under his breath. It appeared the paparazzi got what they needed and finally let up.

"We'll wait inside the lobby for you." Carl opened the back door.

"Okay. It might take me a minute to find a parking spot."

"No problem." Carl stepped out onto the sidewalk, pausing for Keith.

Once they shut the door, the stretch limousine pulled away. They headed inside and Carl inhaled deeply as if the worst was over.

"You okay with this, Carl?" Keith smoothed his hand up Carl's chest as it stood exposed from his unbuttoned shirt and jacket.

"Yes." Carl kissed Keith. "What do you want to do with him?"

"Play?"

"Fuck him?"

"Oh, no way."

"Oh?" Carl tilted his head.

"I just want him to suck one of us or just watch as we do it together."

"He needs to get off as well, Keith."

"Give him a hand job or let him jack off or something."

Carl was relieved that Keith did not want to screw the man. It meant a lot to him that Keith still wanted that act to be exclusive.

In a few minutes, the driver appeared at the lobby entrance.

"Wow." Carl got his first good look at the man. He rushed to open the door. "Come in."

"Hey." The man smiled wickedly. "Thanks for this. I mean it. It's really incredible."

Keith pushed the button for the elevator. "What's your name?"

"Scott Baldwin."

"Any relation to Alec?" Keith asked, entering the elevator.

"No." Scott lowered his dark lashes shyly. "I wish."

There was an awkward silence as they ascended. Carl wondered what the hell you said to a man you invited in for novelty sex.

Once inside their condo, Carl took off his sports coat and tossed it over a chair. "Anyone want a drink?" When he spun around, Carl found Keith helping Scott remove his black jacket. "Okay," Carl muttered nervously, "drinks later." Pausing, seeing Scott's tanned, hairless, muscled chest being revealed from his uniform, Carl licked his lips in delight. "Shall we go to the bedroom?"

Leading the way, Carl turned down the blankets, took out the rubbers and lube, and switched on a small table lamp that sat beside the bed.

Seeing both men getting undressed, Carl shook himself out of his daydream and slid the unfastened shirt off his body.

Keith was naked first. Immediately, he stood in front of Scott, waiting for him to finish. The moment Scott had shed his last article of clothing, Keith touched Scott's pectoral muscles. The sight of their contact sent Carl's cock upwards.

Keith reached out to him. Carl hurried to join the party.

With Keith's arm around Scott's waist, Keith drew Carl into a kiss. Their three torsos connected in an electric exchange. As Carl sucked on Keith's tongue, Scott ran his hand along Carl's lower back to his bottom. The touch of a strange man sent chills rushing all over Carl's skin.

As he and Keith kissed passionately, Scott embraced them, sliding his large erection between Carl and Keith's bodies as they embraced.

It was intense and the buzz of Scott witnessing their contact was lighting up something strong in Carl. Carl could only wonder how Keith was feeling. This was one of Keith's fantasies.

As Scott's hand glided down Carl's crack, Carl imagined Scott doing the same to Keith. Scott's warm finger pressed against Carl's ass. It sent a shockwave over his body and he groaned in longing.

While Keith's tongue dueled with his, Scott licked Carl's cheek, moving towards their mouths. A third tongue made its way into the kissing. Carl's cock jerked with the thrill, knocking into Keith's as it did.

Keith parted from the connection, panting so hard Carl thought he would hyperventilate. Carl could tell this type of contact aroused Keith to the point of swooning.

Carl decided to take the lead since no one was doing much

more than gasping for breath at the moment. He directed Keith to their bed and urged him down on it.

"What do you want me to do?" Scott asked, obviously concerned with their expectations.

"Only what you're comfortable doing," Carl replied softly.

"That doesn't leave out much." Scott grinned wickedly.

"Suck me while he fucks me," Keith panted, fisting his own cock.

"My pleasure." Scott stroked himself as he waited.

Carl used a rubber. Even though he and Keith had one bout of unprotected sex, everything in Carl's body said "safe" at the moment. He rolled one on, covering it with lube. Once he had some on his fingers, he urged Keith up on his hands and knees and smoothed the gel inside Keith's ass.

Keith hissed a breath of air through his teeth in pleasure.

"Let me get under both of you." Scott touched Keith's arm.

As they repositioned themselves, Scott lay face up on the bed between Keith's knees. Carl ended up straddling Scott's hips, and if he had the urge, he could easily squat down on his protruding dick and get fucked. Shaking himself out of that fantasy, Carl knelt upright to get in position to enter Keith. The logistics were trying for a moment until everyone could reach their target. As he held Keith's hips, Carl was dying to see what Scott was doing. Right before he penetrated his lover, he leaned down and caught sight of Scott holding Keith's cock at the base and pointing it at his mouth. Scott's other hand was fisting his own dick. Seeing the last unsatisfied member had a method of release, Carl aimed his cock at Keith's ass and pushed in.

Instantly, Keith moaned a deep long whimper of ecstasy.

Imagining Keith's cock getting sucked at the same time as he fucked him made Carl so hot he couldn't believe it.

Clamped onto Keith's hips, Carl thrust inside him, sliding in effortlessly and knowing holding back would be impossible.

~

Keith was getting his dick sucked by a god as he was screwed by Carl. Life just couldn't get any better than this. And he loved Carl for letting him have this fantasy. It showed Keith how confident Carl was about their relationship. There was no cheating, no sneaking around behind the other one's back. They shared this experience. And Keith would have it no other way.

Opening his eyes, looking down at Scott who was sucking him with so much confidence and skill, Keith knew he was going to come quickly. Behind him, Carl was grunting and thrusting to his heart's content. Imagining Scott masturbating below them both, Keith began to spin from the stimulation. "Oh, Carl...Carl..." he crooned, seductively. At his words Scott lit up and drew him deeper and faster into his mouth. Carl amped up his thrusting at Keith's sexual moans as well. Keith knew dirty talk would send them all reeling. "Carl, fuck me. Fuck me! Oh, Christ, Scott! Suck it, suck it hard!"

Under them Scott began jerking his hips as his come splashed against Keith's thigh. Feeling that hot spatter, Keith shut his eyes and pushed deeper into Scott's boiling hot mouth. "*Ahhh! Christ!*" Keith came, feeling the sensation pique as his body quivered from head to toe. Behind him, Carl's cock shivered and throbbed like mad as he came. Carl's deep, masculine grunting filled the room while Carl's come filled Keith's body. Below him Scott lapped at Keith gently as they both recovered. Hanging his head down to catch his breath, Keith felt Carl pulling out of him slowly.

When he did, Keith crawled backwards and dropped on top of Scott to relax his tired arms.

Scott curled around him and hugged him tight. As Carl disappeared into the bathroom to clean up, Keith tried to breathe normally.

The moment Carl returned he climbed next to them on the

bed and they snuggled together tightly. In silence they calmed down, running their hands over each others' dew-coated skin.

Scott opened up his arms to unite Carl and Keith over him. As Keith leaned up on his side next to Scott, he reached across Scott to his lover. Carl met Keith's lips and kissed him as Scott watched from below.

"You two are perfect for each other," Scott whispered. "Thank you for sharing your love with me."

Keith parted from Carl's lips and smiled down at Scott. "Thank you for playing with us."

"Believe me. It's my pleasure." Scott's beaming grin turned from one to the other.

Meeting Carl's sated, weary smile, Keith reached out to stroke his hair. "I love you, babe."

"I love you too, Keith."

A wooziness filling his body, Keith closed his eyes and fell asleep in a bed overflowing with men.

Chapter Seven

As they were getting ready to go to the studio, Keith's mobile phone rang. Rushing to find it, digging through last night's clothing, Keith scooped it out of his trouser pocket. "Hello?"

"Keith? Adam Lewis."

"Hi, Adam." Keith twisted back to see Carl with his coffee mug to his lips, watching him. Scott had left after their love session last night.

"Jeff Palmer called. He said there's a nice front page spread of you and Carl in the tabloids."

"Oh?"

"Yes, you and your model girlfriends made a big splash last night."

The irony wasn't lost on Keith. "Great."

"It is great, Keith. Keep it up. It'll send all those gay rumors out the window and the two of you will be just fine."

Keith sat down on the sofa with a sigh. "Adam, do you truly believe if Carl and I came out we'd be in trouble?"

"Yes."

Blinking at the blunt response, Keith felt crushed. "I was hoping you would say maybe not."

"Keith, we've had this discussion several times. What can I say? If you want to take the chance, fine. But when *Forever Young* ends, so will your options for any major motion picture role, particularly if it's for romantic leading man."

"You told me I was too pretty for most parts anyway, Adam." Keith stared at Carl as he spoke.

"With this show added to your credentials, it will make a difference. I already have some producers sniffing around."

"For me?" Keith pressed his fingers to his chest.

"Yes. I've received several enquiries this morning since the early press released the photos of you with a woman. It was that easy, Keith. The minute you appeared straight, the phone began ringing."

"Adam, that is unreal. And to be honest, quite fucking sad."

Carl sat down next to Keith, rubbing his knee affectionately.

"I know. It sucks. But be prepared for a movie offer, hopefully in the next week."

Keith skin tingled at the thought. "I would love to do a movie, Adam."

"I know, babe. Just keep up the act for the public and they will roll in for you and Carl."

"Okay. We'll try." Keith wondered if they took a big chance last night going to that gay bar. Well, he didn't have to wonder. They had taken a chance.

"How were the women Jeff set you up with? Tolerable?"

"Yes. They were. They seemed really sympathetic." Keith caressed Carl's rough jaw.

"Good. Jeff's great at this game. Let him lead you."

"I will."

"Okay, let me go. I'll let you know about any secure offers if I get any."

"Thanks, Adam." Keith hung up and stared at his lover. "The papers had us on their front covers with Holly and Jade."

Carl nodded, urging Keith to keep going.

"And..." Keith tried to sound excited. "The minute we were exposed for being straight," he caressed Carl's jaw, "Adam started getting phone calls for me."

Shrugging, Carl sighed, "It's exactly what we were supposed

to do, babe. I'm really happy it worked."

"We can't go to the club anymore, Carl."

"No. No way. Hey, we had a night of good gay fun. It'll last for a while."

"Wasn't Scott terrific?"

"He was. He was perfect for us. I could tell he had no expectations for anything in the future and just enjoyed the moment."

"Thanks again, Carl, for letting me do that."

"I enjoyed it." Carl hugged him.

Kissing Carl's cheek, Keith savored the cuddle.

"We do have to get going." Carl broke the embrace.

"Yes. Let's go." Keith followed Carl to bedroom to gather their wallets and make sure they had everything they needed for the day.

~

As Carl entered the studio, headed to their set, he found a copy of the weekly tabloid resting on a folding chair. Picking it up, Carl stared at the front page. *Forever Young's Gorgeous Gay Couple Out With Their Ladies for a Night on the Town.* Carl held the photo up to show Keith.

"Amazing what being seen with women can do for your reputation."

"Perception." Carl tossed the paper back on the chair. "It's a game of perceptions, Keith." About to say something about that crazy night, Carl stopped short when Charlotte approached them.

"Good morning, boss," Keith greeted her.

She scowled down at the paper. "Are you trying to ruin the show?"

"Excuse me?" Carl choked at the insult. "We're trying to salvage our reputations, Ms. Deavers."

"What I'm saying to you right now comes not only from me but directly from the producers, Derek Dixon and Will Markham. Do you realize how many fans will be upset with your straight act?"

"Act?" Keith refuted. "We're not acting straight, Charlotte. We act gay, remember?"

"Do you two really have to play that stupid game with me?"

"Come on, Charlotte," Carl chided. "Don't make this an issue. You know this business well enough to realize we need a career after *Forever Young* goes bye-bye."

"And you, Carl Bronson, know well enough that a show with the type of ratings we're getting can go on for a decade. Unless something or someone, fucks it up."

Carl checked the expression on Keith's face. It was one of disbelief. Throwing up his hands in frustration, Carl asked, "What the hell do you want us to do, Charlotte? We have both been advised by our agents to take care not to get a gay reputation in the tabloids."

"You know how long I've been in the business, Carl?" Charlotte folded her arms across her chest.

Carl began calculating the number. Before he wagered a guess, Charlotte announced, "Fifteen, Carl."

"Okay…" He assumed there'd be more to her reply.

"On *The Ties that Bind* I had to convince our viewers that the two main characters were into bondage. So that meant they couldn't be seen in their Sunday best at bible study."

"Charlotte," Keith shook his head in admonishment, "give us a break."

She continued, "No, I won't. Listen to me, you two. The show's demographics are women and gay men. Got it? If all those women out there see you two as happy straight couples, they will turn off you. And don't even get me started on what the gay viewers will think. They'll be miffed, and that's putting it politely."

"Charlotte…" Carl wanted to speak in their defense.

She held up her hand to stop him. "You want this show to be ended by this season? Fine. Show the world you're madly in love with two boney fashion models. You'll be looking for work by summer."

"That's crap and you know it." Carl hated being in this position. "You want me to list the actors who have previously acted in gay roles, but are straight? It did nothing to cancel the show. *Will and Grace*? Hello? Two straight men playing gay guys. Eight years, Charlotte. Eight years that show ran."

"Don't talk to me about *Will and Grace*," she scoffed. "One cliché gay character and another who never had a steady boyfriend? That show did nothing for gay men."

"What?" Keith objected, "Nothing for gay men? Are you kidding me? Every person who watched that show wanted to believe that gay guys were okay in their book."

Charlotte glared at Keith. "They were sterile depictions of cartoon gay men. Don't get me started." She checked her watch. "We have to get taping. I just want you two to think long and hard about what you're doing. Do some research, will you? Stop listening to the money-grubbing advice of your agents and imagine awards coming from every corner, including the GLAAD media awards."

"The what?" Carl tilted his head curiously.

"The Gay and Lesbian Alliance Against Defamation."

"Where does she come up with this shit?" Keith asked Carl incredulously.

"Enough." Charlotte waved her hand in annoyance. "Get ready. We have a show to do."

Carl nudged Keith and headed to the wardrobe area.

Keith murmured, "We can't fucking win."

"I know." Carl greeted Melvin and started changing his clothing.

"How are you boys doing this morning?" Mel asked, hanging

their clothing selections on two racks.

"Good. How are you, Mel?" Carl replied, taking off his shirt.

"I'm just fine and dandy. Did you enjoy your night of dancing with the boys?"

Carl jerked his head to Keith who appeared pale and panic-stricken. "I don't know what you're talking about." Carl pulled a shirt off of a hanger and slid it on.

"Don't worry. I'll never tell." Mel helped Carl with his collar and buttons.

"Were you there?" Keith whispered.

"No. But many of my friends were."

"We're dead." Keith's mouth tightened to a straight line.

"Not necessarily," Mel asserted. "Listen to me, boys. Personally, I think what you did in that club will boost your ratings. Look, gay men aren't stupid. They know damn well you have to play the straight game."

Carl stepped out of his jeans and into a pair of black slacks. "Do we?" Carl asked seriously. "Do we really have to play it?"

"I am so confused my head hurts." Keith tucked his shirt in as he stepped into leather loafers.

"There are no easy answers." Melvin fixed Keith's shirt collar.

"Oh no," Carl replied sarcastically, "there are plenty of easy answers, just no sane ones."

When they had finished dressing, Melvin drew both of their attention. "Follow your heart."

"And lose your career," Carl added.

"Maybe not. Carl, it's becoming a new trend in Hollywood. Men are braving the backlash and stepping up to the plate."

Carl glanced at Keith for his response.

"And," Mel announced, "the more men there are who do come out? The easier it will get."

"I'm no sacrificial lamb," Carl argued. "Let someone else risk life and limb."

Mel shrugged. "It's your decision. No one can make it but you." Before they headed to Ken for their make-up, Mel prompted, "But if you think having headlines in the tabloids about your fake women is helping your popularity? Think again."

Thanking Mel under his breath, Carl walked beside Keith to a waiting Ken. Silent as they were powdered and their hair was brushed, Carl couldn't rid the sinking feeling in his gut. Maybe this should never have happened in the first place. He and Keith should have remained friends and never crossed the line from make-believe to reality. It was a mistake. The ruin to their careers was looming like a thundercloud over a picnic.

Finally, on their way to the set and a waiting Charlotte and crew, Carl tried to remember his lines. With the distraction of the outside world beating him down, acting was becoming as difficult as lying to himself.

Seeing Charlotte's tired expression, Carl knew the decisions he and Keith were making affected everything around them, including their performance and the longevity of their hit show.

"Okay," Charlotte stated, certainly not with her usual zeal, "we'll do a camera rehearsal. Go get in place."

Carl moved to his spot on the set, shaking his body to loosen it up as if he were about to sprint in a race. He forced himself to get into character.

~

Keith was devastated. He thought Adam knew the right thing to do for his career, and Keith was positive Adam was looking out for his future. But…at what expense? If he was exposed as a fraud to the public wasn't that worse than just coming out?

Struggling to remember his lines for the upcoming scene, Keith had to stop thinking about the problems they had and focus.

"Living room scene. Camera rehearsal. Action!"

Spinning around, Keith gazed at Carl. "It's not my fault! Blame your meddling mother!"

"My mother? You're the one who outed us at the party, Dennis. I told you it was risky to kiss anywhere that wasn't private."

Keith's expression softened. He closed the gap between them and held Carl's hands. "I couldn't help it, Troy. Do you know how hard it is to pretend I don't love you?"

"I know, Dennis." Carl withdrew one hand so he could caress Keith's cheek.

Keith embraced Carl, connecting their hips. "I hate lying. I hate pretending we're not a couple."

"Me too. I just don't see a way out of this alive, Dennis."

Just the contact of their bodies sent Keith's cock vertical. He couldn't prevent the love and attraction he and Carl shared. Why should he try to stop loving him? Wanting him?

"I do." Keith pressed his dick against Carl, craving him to feel how hard he had gotten. "Let's just bare ourselves in public. Throw caution to the wind. Other men have done it, other men have survived."

"That's easier said than done." Carl rubbed his erection against Keith's, obviously knowing Keith yearned for the turn on.

"No. It's easier done."

Carl cradled the back of Keith's head and drew him to his lips.

The touch of their mouths sent shivers all over Keith's body. Taking their time, making it count, Keith made damn sure their tongue kiss was visible for the camera. Parting after a long moment, Keith whispered, "We have nothing to be ashamed of, Troy. How can love be wrong or embarrassing?"

"You're so brave, Dennis. I don't know if I can do it."

Keith smoothed his hand down Carl's back to his ass, cupping it affectionately. "Do it with me."

Carl swung Keith up into his arms, holding him like a baby.

Keith wrapped around Carl's neck, sucking at his mouth as Carl dipped them sensually. When they parted lips, Carl hissed, "For you, I would do anything."

"Good. Then it's settled."

Carl carried Keith to their bedroom set.

"Cut!"

Once the scene ended, Carl set Keith on his feet. The moment he did, Keith looked back at the cameras to see Charlotte's reaction. "Carl. Who are those men?"

Carl spun to look. "Shit. The producer, Derek Dixon, and co-producer, Will Markham." Carl reached back and gave Keith's hand a quick squeeze in support.

Charlotte went over some corrections for the cameras as the men waited. Keith didn't catch eyes with either of the big wigs. He'd never seen them at a taping before and had a feeling their presence was a direct reaction to the tabloids running the story of his and Carl's new model girlfriends. Charlotte's warning rang out in his head.

"Okay. Again. Get into position."

Seeing Charlotte's pinched expression, Keith knew he and Carl weren't the only ones under pressure. The buck stopped with Charlotte.

"Living room scene. First taping. Take one. Action!"

~

After two more attempts they had completed the scene to Charlotte's satisfaction. Keith followed Carl to the refreshment table before anyone could say anything to them. Charlotte was having a private conversation with the two producers behind the cameras.

"You realize we're in for another lecture." Carl sipped from a bottle of water.

"I do. Carl, you tell me what the right thing to do is."

"I have no clue."

"I want to come out. I honestly do, Carl. I want us to be able to go to the awards ceremonies hand in hand. I want us to go to gay bars if we want to. I also want to show our support for the gay community. But."

"But." Carl knew, Keith didn't have to reiterate it.

"Gentlemen?"

Keith spun around. The imposing producers of their show were standing behind them.

Immediately, Carl reached out his hand for a shake. "Mr. Dixon, Mr. Markham, so nice to see you."

Keith had never met them before but he certainly knew them by their reputation. "Sir." He extended his hand and repeated to each, "Nice to finally meet you."

"Can we have a word?" Derek gestured to a private room off of the set.

Gulping the rest of his juice to get rid of the glass, Keith's nerves kick in. It felt like a reprimand at school and he was about to get scolded by the principal.

Carl opened a door to a room Keith had never entered previously. It was pitch dark until Carl lit the overhead light. A table surrounded by chairs filled the space. Once the four of them had entered, Will closed the door for complete privacy.

"Sit." Derek gestured.

Instinctively, Carl and Keith sat next to each other opposite the two older men.

Derek opened the button of his suit jacket. He was the only one in a business suit. Will wore casual jeans and a cotton shirt.

"Charlotte told me she's spoken to you already." Derek rested his elbows on the table, his hands pressed together as if he were praying.

"Yes, sir." Carl nodded.

Keith knew these men held his and Carl's acting fates in their hands. He reached for Carl under the table and curled his fingers around Carl's.

"We realize when a career is new, a young man will be cautious before being open about his sexuality."

Keith kept his mouth sealed shut. He knew what they were going to say. Charlotte already had. Perhaps their director thought they needed more persuasion from the big guns.

"And neither myself or Will want to tell you what to do."

Keith doubted that very much. He felt Carl's grip tighten on his hand.

"But saying that," Derek lowered his tone and allowed his arms to relax on the table in front of him. "Our ratings depend upon perceptions. And I totally understand if you don't want to come out as gay men. Again, this is your personal decision. My concern is in the overt heterosexual display orchestrated for the tabloids."

The grasp on his fingers became painful, but Keith knew this conversation would be murder.

Will Markham spoke up. "We would prefer it if you didn't play the tabloid game. Perhaps you could just refrain from verifying their suspicions without flaunting a fake heterosexual relationship in the media."

Keith felt the pause in conversation like pain. What did they want him and Carl to say? *Yes? Out me? Give you the ratings you deserve at the expense of...what?*

Again Derek expressed, "Do you see where we're coming from? We have been told by an inside source that this show may be getting six Emmy nominations, and that includes best actor and best supporting actor in a drama series." He paused before he pointed. "You two."

The thrill of a nomination made Keith feel like screaming in joy. Instead he chewed his lip nervously.

"But," Derek continued, "public perception can ruin your chances. You could easily sabotage your own careers by rubbing out the sweet reputations you now have with the label of liar. Or fraud."

It was obvious to Keith suddenly that both of their producers knew they were a gay couple. There was no getting around that fact.

Keith looked into the stern expression on Will Markham's face. The man was very good looking, possibly in his forties, with no wedding ring on his finger. Gay? Keith could only assume. Conservatively dressed and groomed, fifty-something, Derek Dixon wore a gold band. Keith guessed he was married with children.

"If you come across as dishonest, we will lose out on those awards, and in turn the series will not be as long lived as we would like it to be." Derek set his gaze on Carl.

Keith felt Carl's body tremble under the scrutiny. What these men were asking of them seemed monumental.

Will cleared his throat to get their attention. "Derek and I hoped to run this series, at the very least, for five years, eager for eight or nine. The kudos we're getting for our depiction of real gay men has been overwhelming. Think of the contradiction in the media if it comes out you two are faking straight relationships..." he paused as if for effect, then stressed, "and are lovers in real life."

A trickle of sweat ran down Keith's temple in the stuffy room. He dabbed at it discreetly.

Another protracted pause engulfed them. Finally, seemingly irritated by the silence, Derek asked directly, "Don't either of you have anything to say for yourselves? Or do all your lines have to be written for you?"

"Ouch!" Keith choked in surprise. "That's not very nice."

"Then say something. Don't just sit there like pretty mannequins." Derek reclined in his chair.

Keith disengaged his hand from Carl's and placed his forearms on the table in front of him. "I understand everything you are saying. Both Carl and I do. Do you have any idea how long we have agonized over this?"

Neither man answered, obviously allowing Keith his chance to vent.

"We each have agents representing us." Keith glanced at Carl whose face was stern. "Adam Lewis and Cole Rossi. Both of our agents warned us about coming out to the public. Adam said very clearly that if we did, after your—*our* show either ended or is cancelled, we'd be left out in the cold."

Again Keith didn't get a response. He looked to Carl for some back up.

And Carl replied, "Name me one leading man in the film industry that has come out as gay."

Keith waited. No one named anyone.

Derek sighed deeply before he answered. "We're not asking you to come out."

"In a way you are." Keith leaned closer to them over the table. "If we don't deny we're gay, be seen with women, then by default, because of the characters we play, people will assume we are gay."

"Nonsense," Will scoffed.

"Are you gay?" Keith asked him boldly.

"Yes." Will's eyes became raw as he glared at them.

"Is that common knowledge?" Carl replied.

Derek grew angry. "What the heck does Will's sexuality have to do with this? He's not in front of the camera, you are. Stop changing the topic."

"Are you out?" Keith insisted.

"Yes." Will grimaced slightly at the declaration.

It took the wind out of Keith's righteous sails. The point was moot suddenly. Rubbing his tired eyes, Keith stated, "Carl, it's no use."

Derek held their attention once again. "Do you want this show to remain on the air?"

"Yes," both Keith and Carl answered in stereo.

"Fine. If you want *Forever Young* to be long lasting, and for Troy Wright and Dennis Jason to continue loving and showing the world that gay men are not something to shun, then all we ask is that you drop the het act. I'll repeat, we don't expect you to come out and declare yourselves gay. No one would expect that of you. Just stop pretending you have plastic women in your life. Go about your business as usual. Work, socialize, play, just stop manufacturing a relationship that doesn't exist."

Will maintained, "You're not fooling anyone. On the contrary, you look foolish. It gives you both a ring of deceit that we don't want tainting a number one show."

"Are you guaranteeing we will be in the show until its conclusion?" Keith wanted some reassurances of work. The last thing he needed was to be branded a gay pariah and exiled to the washed-up actor's unemployment line at the meager age of twenty-six.

"Yes." Both Derek and Will nodded confidently. "You two make the damn show. If we cut either one of you, it's finished. While this show runs, you will have work. Period. No question. We did a Neilson poll and by those stats you two as the gay couple Troy and Dennis are the all-time favorite in nighttime drama. The number was overwhelming."

"Wow." Keith sat back to digest it.

"Don't either of you look at the fan sites?" Will asked.

"We checked out a few. Including that YouTube thing." Carl adjusted his position on his chair so his leg was against Keith's.

"Oh, that." Will smiled impishly.

Will's smug expression gave Keith a sinking sensation. "Did you sanction that clip?"

Derek and Will exchanged cheeky glances.

"No!" Carl admonished. "Tell me you did not create that video."

"Our dicks showed on that thing!" Keith was not amused.

"We didn't create it, but we knew about it." Will seemed to be trying to wipe the smirk off his amused face.

"Come on, guys," Keith pleaded. "Don't do things like that behind our backs."

"Oh?" Derek asked, "Would you have allowed us to put up an x-rated video with your blessing?"

"Why did you do that?" Carl moaned.

"I'll repeat what I already said," Will sounded hostile suddenly, "do either of you check the internet for feedback?"

"What are we supposed to be looking for?" Keith fought to hold back his anger. "I'm scared shitless to read what people are saying about us."

"That's a mistake." Derek loosened his necktie in the warm room. "If you did, you'd see the support for the two of you as a couple."

"I feel like I'm on a merry-go-round." Keith rubbed his forehead as it began to ache.

"All right." Will waved his hand. "You get the idea. We don't have to keep pounding it in."

Derek stood, moving out his chair. "It's not a lot to ask, guys. Just be yourselves."

Keith and Carl rose up. Keith was anxious to get out of the close room. "Would you both promise to put in a good word for us if and when this show is cancelled?"

"If you co-operate, yes." Will scooted his chair back under the table.

"Geez, that sounds like blackmail," Carl said.

Keith elbowed him to shut up. Luckily, the men had a sense of humor.

Before the door was opened, Will joked, "Yes, blackmail. Either you come clean or you're fired."

"Ha. Ha." Keith narrowed his eyes at Will.

"At least we're not asking you for sex." Will met Keith's eyes directly, "like some sleazy Hollywood agents."

"Adam never does that." Keith felt his skin go red from embarrassment.

"Oh? Then you know nothing about his deceased business partner, Jack Turner," Will scoffed.

"I know about it." Keith realized he wasn't the only man in LA battling with his image. "Adam Lewis is straight up. He would never ask for that."

"Straight up? Lewis?" Derek laughed. "Tell his gay lawyer boyfriend that."

"All right." Keith had enough.

"Bottom line, Keith. Who are you willing to take career advice from? A man like Lewis with questionable couch practices, or two powerful television producers with your and the show's best interest at heart?" Derek opened the door. "Good day, gentlemen. Oh, and by the way, nice job earlier on the taping. You two burn up the screen."

"Yes," Will emphasized, "good work. The two of you play a very convincing gay couple."

The look of irony on their faces was killing Keith.

Carl mumbled goodbye as they left. Once the sound of their footsteps vanished, Carl dropped back down to a chair to recuperate from the meeting.

Keith sat next to him, cuddling around him. "Why is our life so damn complicated?"

"I don't know." Carl rubbed his eyes with his index finger and thumb.

"What the hell are we supposed to do now?" Keith leaned his chin on Carl's arm.

"You're asking me?" Carl scoffed at the absurdity. "I feel like taffy! Go straight! Go gay! Come out! Stay in!"

"I wish we had a crystal ball. I would really like to see what happens to our careers after this series ends."

"Yeah, but if we don't do as they ask, it'll end very quickly. And to be honest, Keith? I like this show. I don't want it to end.

You do realize we get paid well to kiss and play together on TV. Where the hell are we going to get another job like that?"

Keith allowed Carl to turn so they were face to face. "I bet it must be nice to get paid for screwing men."

"Screwing?" Carl raised his eyebrow.

"If we're through in mainstream TV after this show, I could do gay porno movies."

Carl cracked up. "I do love you."

Keith leaned in for a kiss. "I love you too, handsome."

Chapter Eight

Driving back to the condo after the shoot, Carl's mobile phone rang. Shifting in his seat to get at his pocket, Carl removed it and answered it while Keith watched him from the passenger's side. "Hello?"

"Carl? Cole here."

"Hiya, Cole." Carl glanced at Keith quickly. "My agent," he mouthed silently.

"I've a few offers on my desk for you and I wondered when you would be available for a chat."

"Anything good?"

"Yes. One is for a part in an action film."

"Lead?" Carl stopped for a red light.

"No. Supporting. But a nice size role. Great exposure into the big screen."

"Great." Carl winked at Keith.

"Ever since that front page in the tabloid press with you holding a woman, it's like the floodgates have opened."

Carl's smile dropped. "Oh?"

"Yeah. It's as if they were all hesitant to hire a gay man, and suddenly with the sight of you and a woman together, they seemed to breathe a collective sigh of relief and the offers appeared."

Without a sound, Carl mouthed, "Fuck!"

Keith grabbed his knee in response to that silent expletive.

Moving as the light changed, Carl muttered, "When do you want me to come by."

"Sooner the better."

Carl looked over at Keith. "You mind a detour before we head home?"

"Of course not."

"I can be there in five," Carl said into the phone.

"Great. See you then."

Carl disconnected and tossed the mobile into the cup holder on the console.

"What?" Keith asked as Carl rubbed at his jaw stubble.

"My agent said the minute we were photographed with Jade and Holly, he was flooded with offers."

Keith slumped down in the bucket seat and covered his face in agony.

"Taffy," Carl sighed. "Fucking salt water taffy."

"I don't fucking believe any of this." Keith balled up his fists and almost screamed, "Why does who we fuck in the bedroom matter?"

Carl laughed sadly. "Good question."

"Aren't we still the same men? The same actors?"

"Hell no. If we're gay we don't have testicles and can't have a romantic part with a woman. How can you be a man if you don't have any balls between your legs? Don't you know that? Being gay in Hollywood turns men into eunuchs."

"What's the offered part?"

"In some action movie. Gay men don't do action movies, Keith," Carl ranted bitterly. "Oh, no. If you're gay you turn off straight men, right? So, if James Bond was played by an out gay man? No sales. That's what they all think."

"What do you think?"

"I think it's a load of crap."

"Oh? And since that piece in the tabloids? Offers for movies? You call that crap? Who are you kidding?"

"I don't know who we're kidding anymore. My head is upside down at the moment. I wish we did have that crystal ball, babe. It would help."

Carl pulled into a lot of a high-rise building. Shutting off the engine, Carl opened the door as Keith asked, "You want me to wait here?"

"No."

Keith acknowledged him and got out, meeting him on the sidewalk in front of the lobby entrance.

Walking through the large glossy atrium to the wall of elevators, Carl wanted to hold Keith's hand in a gesture of affection and it annoyed him he couldn't.

Once they were inside the seclusion of the elevator, it was a different story. The minute the door closed, Carl pushed Keith against the wall and practically mounted him.

A grunt of surprise emerged from Keith until he wrapped around Carl and sucked back at his mouth. The bell rang to alert them of their arrival. Carl pushed back from Keith's hot body and wiped the taste of Keith's mouth off his own lips gently. "I love you."

"Me too!" Keith announced happily, touching Carl's arm as the doors parted.

"This way." Carl tilted his head towards a hallway with one side paneled with large glass panes, over plush mauve carpet. Original lithographs lined the corridor and huge potted trees accented the pale pink walls.

Carl opened an office door and stepped in. "Hello, Paula."

"Hiya, Carl!" An attractive young woman waved at him from behind her desk. "I'll tell Cole you're here."

"Great." Carl watched as she gave his lover a once over. *Whatever. It's no secret Keith and I are friends.*

"Cole? Carl Bronson is here." She hung up. "Go right in, sweetie."

"Thanks." Carl reached out for Keith to join him.

~

Keith wondered if Mr. Rossi had even more clout in Hollywood than Adam Lewis. The office was dripping with expensive trinkets and artifacts from a lifetime of exotic traveling.

After Carl greeted the gray-haired gentleman, he gestured back to Keith. "You know my co-star? Keith O'Leary?"

Keith shook Mr. Rossi's hand. "Nice to meet you."

"Yes. I've heard a lot about you." Mr. Rossi did not smile when he said that, releasing Keith's hand abruptly. "Carl. Have a seat."

Trying not to interfere, Keith moved to a chair against one wall and looked into a glass case with strange, carved, wooden African idols in it.

"Here's one I highly recommend." Cole pushed paperwork at Carl. "Blockbuster summer movie about a superhero."

"Am I a good guy or a bad guy?" Carl appeared amused.

"Good. You're the second banana."

"Really? Like Robin to Batman?"

"Yes."

Keith felt Mr. Rossi's eyes dart to him with discomfort. Perhaps Carl's agent was trying to decide if Carl was gay after all. Maybe seeing them together gave him the idea that the cover story in the tabloid was just that. A cover.

Cole added, "It's going to begin filming during your summer break. No conflict with your cable drama whatsoever."

"Where will it be filmed?"

"Here in LA."

"Good." Carl flipped the pages of the paperwork, a contented smile on his lips.

"This one's for a guest spot on Leno." Cole kept handing Carl paperwork. "This one's for advertising men's underwear in

Japan."

Carl laughed, looking back at Keith in amusement.

Keith tried to smile at him even though Mr. Rossi made him feel uneasy. It was as if Keith was preventing the two of them from talking candidly.

"Just look them over. The audition for the film includes the date, time, and script. That's the big money offer. The rest are just fun extras."

"Okay, Cole." Carl smiled sweetly at him.

Finally Cole appeared to be unable to contain his thoughts. "Carl."

"Yes?"

"You are dating a woman, right?"

Carl whipped his head around to Keith.

What the hell do you want from me? Keith tried to communicate his distress at the topic.

As if making a command decision, Carl replied, "Yes."

"Good. I'm sorry, Carl, but I think if you weren't seen on that latest weekly tabloid with a model on your arm, I wouldn't be handing you any of these offers."

"I know, Cole."

"Give them a look over, and get back to me."

"I will." Carl stood, shaking Cole's hand.

"Bye." Keith waved weakly.

"Goodbye, Mr. O'Leary."

It was said as a scold, and if Carl couldn't hear it, Keith would be amazed.

"Bye, Paula." Carl smiled sweetly at Cole's assistant.

"See ya, Carl. Bye!" she addressed Keith.

"See ya." Keith waved at her.

Once they were in the hall, Keith grumbled, "He hates me."

"What?" Carl tucked the paperwork under his arm and pushed the down button for the elevator. "He does not."

"Yes. He does. I'm the ruin of his top star."

"Shut up."

They entered the elevator, and since they weren't alone, they behaved.

Just as they hit the sunshine and approached Carl's black Corvette, Keith's mobile phone rang. As he climbed into the passenger seat, Keith answered. "Hello?"

"Hey, Keith. It's Adam Lewis."

"Hi, Adam." Keith laughed at the irony. "Let me guess. Since we've come out as heterosexual men you have offers."

"How did you guess?"

"I'm a genius." Keith closed the car door and gave Carl a pained look. "Actually, we're sitting in Carl's car outside his agent's office with his own handful of scripts."

"I told you."

"Adam, we've got a serious problem." Keith rubbed his hand over Carl's thigh as he started the car.

"Oh?"

"The producers, Derek Dixon and Will Markham want us to stop pretending we're straight."

"Crap."

"Ya think?" Keith tried to laugh but it came out like a cough. "Rock, hard place, Adam."

"Keith, their interest is in their drama, period."

"We know that. But it may be the difference between working one season on it or eight."

"Yes. I understand."

"What the hell are we supposed to do, Adam?"

"Where are you guys? Are you anywhere near Malibu?"

"Yes. Why?"

"Come by."

"Your house?" Keith shook Carl's leg for him to stop putting the car in gear for a moment.

"Yes. Come to my house. Let's have a discussion about this."

"Okay."

"See you soon? You know my home address right?"

"Give it to me again." Keith repeated it out loud as he did. Carl nodded he got it. "Okay, Adam. We'll be there as soon as we can."

"Good."

Keith hung up. "You believe this?"

"No. It's insane."

"At least Adam is gay. Christ, I thought Rossi wanted to murder me for killing your career."

"Why do you say that?"

"He was shooting daggers at me behind your back."

"That fuckhead." Carl entered the main road and headed to the coast.

"Sorry. He was."

"He's slightly old fashioned. I don't think he likes the whole West Hollywood gay thing."

"Asshole."

Carl shrugged. "I wasn't gay when he offered to represent me."

"No. You were just another pretty face," Keith purred, cupping Carl's crotch.

~

They found the correct address. Carl pulled into the long sandy drive and parked. "Well, Adam does very well for himself."

"No kidding." Keith unfastened his seatbelt.

"Beachfront. Nice. Have you ever been here before, Keith?"

"No. Never." Keith exited the car and stood for a moment, looking at the front of the white stucco house.

Carl met him at the walkway leading to the door. "Pretty Jaguar."

Keith turned to see a sleek maroon Jaguar XK in the drive.

Walking to the front door, Keith rang the bell. When a muscular blond answered, Keith gaped at him in awe. "Uh…I'm here to see Adam Lewis?"

"Come on in."

Keith entered the interior and admired the southwestern design. "I'm Keith O'Leary and this is Carl Bronson."

"Yes, I recognize you from *Forever Young*. I'm Jack Larsen, Adam's partner."

Keith took his outstretched hand and relinquished it so his lover could take it next.

"Adam is making margaritas. It's his specialty." Jack gestured to the kitchen. "Adam? Your guests are here."

"Hey!" Adam met Keith's eyes as he entered the room. "Come on in and make yourselves comfy."

"Nice place," Carl announced, looking outside at the view of the ocean.

"Thanks. With or without salt?" Adam held up a glass.

"With," Carl replied.

"Without," Keith said, sitting down on a high stool around the island Adam was working on.

"One with, one without." Adam handed them off as he made them, taking one for himself after Jack had his. "Okay. Talk to me, Keith. What the heck is going on?"

"You want me to leave?" Jack asked, pointing to himself.

"No. Stay." Keith smiled at Jack sweetly. He didn't mind staring at him for a while longer. The man was gorgeous, and built like a damn pro-body builder.

Carl relaxed on the stool next to Keith as Jack leaned against the counter.

"We had a chastising from the producer and co-producer of the show," Keith said, sipping the drink. "Mm. Good one!"

"Thanks," Adam accepted the compliment. "What did they say, Keith?"

"Well, they were very upset at the tabloid photos of me and

Carl with the models Jeff Palmer set us up with. They pretty much told Carl and I that we were going to ruin the ratings if we didn't keep our sexual preference ambiguous."

Adam shook his head sadly. "Typical. Thinking of themselves."

"I don't know about that, Adam." Carl set his drink down on the counter. "If the show can run for almost a decade, then it's easy money for me and Keith. We don't want the series to end prematurely."

"What a choice." Jack dragged one of the chairs from the kitchen table over to sit on.

Keith lost himself momentarily on Jack's massive biceps and forearms before he shook himself back to the conversation. "Yes. Anyway, they pretty much said we can't keep up the charade. And to be honest, Adam? Carl and I hated it. It felt very wrong."

"Okay." Adam shrugged. "Don't do it again."

"But," Carl asked like a complete statement.

"But?" Adam responded. "Take the chance."

"I want to come out, Adam." Keith wiped the margarita off his lips with his index finger. "I want to be free to dance at gay nightclubs. To support the gay community."

Keith caught Adam glance at Carl for his opinion.

After a deep long sigh, Carl shook his head. "I disagree. Adam, I just came from my agent's office with an offer for a blockbuster action movie. Everyone in this room knows if I come out, that offer disappears."

"This sucks." Jack reached to place his empty glass on the counter.

"Welcome to our world." Keith smiled sweetly at the handsome blond.

Jack stood, moving closer to their group. "Adam, you can't tell me it would make that much of a difference to people. What century are we in?"

"Jack..." Adam chided, "we've had this discussion. I've

asked the same question over and over again, and I'll ask it once more. What gay icon do you know doing big summer action packed blockbusters or romances? Hm?"

That shut everyone up.

Gesturing around the room, Adam replied, "I rest my case."

"There has to be a compromise." Carl finished his drink and balanced his glass on the counter.

"Yes," Keith agreed. "Some way we can get our cake and eat it."

Jack cracked up at the comment while Adam smiled wryly and Carl covered his smirk.

"Yeah, wouldn't that be nice." Adam held up the pitcher. "Refills?"

As Keith watched Adam top up their glasses, the doorbell rang. "Are we keeping you from something?" Keith asked.

"No. I have a feeling it's just Mark and Steve." Adam glanced at Jack as he left the room to answer the door.

"Gay couple?" Carl enquired softly.

"Yes. Oh, just ignore Mark. He's liable to get all gushy over meeting you two."

Smiling shyly, Keith replied, "So? I like that."

"Good." Adam winked.

Sipping the second margarita quietly, Keith could hear Jack greeting the men as they came in.

"Whose car is that, Jackie?"

"Come in and see."

Swiveling on the stool, Keith faced the threshold of the living room, waiting to witness their reaction.

The minute one man entered the room, Keith almost fell off his chair. And Adam thought his friend would be all gushy? *Holy Christ!* Keith caught Carl's gaze quickly, assessing his opinion to be the same.

"You're Dennis Jason and Troy Wright from *Forever Young!*"

Keith choked, "And you're British as well?"

"As well as what?"

Jack touched the gorgeous man's shoulder. "Mark, this is Keith O'Leary and Carl Bronson. Guys, this is Mark Richfield and his partner, Steve Miller."

"Hey." Steve waved, managing to get into the kitchen around Mark and Jack who had paused at the doorway. "Margaritas?"

"I'll make more." Adam went into action.

"Do you act?" Keith asked Mark.

"No. I don't." Mark smiled flirtatiously. "Why? You think I'm cute?"

"Don't start, Mark." Steve rolled his eyes. "He's sees handsome men and he gets all ga-ga."

Keith couldn't quite get over Mark Richfield. Tall, lean, athletic, and as pretty as any woman Keith had ever seen. Kissing him would be like having the best of both worlds.

"I like your hair." Keith reached out to touch it.

Mark leaned closer, allowing Keith to run his fingers through its length.

"Is it hot in here?" Carl laughed, fanning himself.

"If it's hot," Mark crooned, "it's because there are two fabulous TV stars in the room."

"Down boy." Steve leaned his elbows on the counter near Adam who was busy mixing more cocktails.

"You see?" Keith pointed to Carl. "This is what it's like to be out."

"Makes me want to have an orgy," Mark purred, thrusting his hips forward.

Keith loved the gesture and gave Mark's full crotch a good inspection. "Jesus. You've got a big dick too?"

"He's the whole damn package," Steve bragged.

Keith glanced back at Carl as if asking permission to have another threesome.

Carl gave Keith a knowing smile. "It's okay with me."

Adam raised his head from his task of stirring a large glass pitcher. "What's okay with you?"

"Nothing," Keith replied, grinning hungrily at Mark.

Jack obviously got it. "Uh, Steve...these adorable young actors have the hots for your man."

"What else is new?" Steve took a bag of pretzels out of a cabinet and opened it, munching on one and passing the rest around. "Christ, your hair's getting long, Adam." Steve tugged on its length. "Soon it'll be as long as Mark's."

Adam gave Jack a smile at the comment.

"Really?" Mark lit up. "You have the hots for me?"

"He's kidding, right?" Keith asked in disbelief. "You're surprised we think you're gorgeous?" Keith took a few pretzels, handed one to Carl and passed the bag to Jack. Holding one out to Mark, Keith asked seductively, "Wanna bite?"

Mark took a quick glance at Steve, leaned closer and nibbled the pretzel from Keith's hand. "Thanks." Mark smiled wickedly as he chewed.

Carl continued to fan himself. "Uh, can someone turn on the air?"

"Jesus!" Keith announced. "You're fucking sexy, Mark Richfield. Err, Steve?" Keith searched around Carl to see him. "Can we borrow your lover?"

"Yeah, right." Steve did not appear amused.

"One hour." Keith held up his index finger.

"Is he kidding me?" Steve stood taller, his hands on his hips.

"Be careful," Mark whispered into Keith's ear, but they all could hear him. "Steve was an LAPD cop. He's very mean."

"I'm not mean." Steve retrieved the bag of pretzels as it came his way again. "I don't want another guy to play with you, Richfield."

Mark leaned his side against Keith's. Keith inhaled Mark's delicious scent deeply.

"He won't let me play, pretty boy," Mark's breath tickled

Keith's ear as he spoke.

Keith was so excited by Mark he was going nuts. "My lover lets me share." Keith wrapped his arm around Mark's waist, hugging him closer.

"Okay!" Adam shouted to break the sexual tension. "Who wants booze?"

"Me." Steve held out a clean glass, unable to wipe the scowl off his face. "Mark, cut it out."

"What am I doing?" Mark held up his hands.

"Keith," Carl admonished, "don't get anyone upset."

"I'm in a room with five of the most gorgeous men I have ever met and I'm supposed to behave? What fucking planet are you all from? Hello? We're gay men? Sex? Anyone for group sex?" Keith turned back to stare at Mark's profile. "Let me see your green eyes again. Carl has green eyes, you know. I love green eyes and dark hair."

"Do you?" Mark sighed.

"I'll bet you give amazing head," Keith hissed.

Mark's eyes blinked wide in shock.

"Oi!" Steve crossed the room and shoved Mark out of Keith's grasp. "I think the flirting has taken a lousy turn in the wrong direction."

Keith smiled at Mark regardless of Steve trying to make his point.

"I don't mind Mark getting some attention," Steve argued, "I'm used to it. But when it gets carried away, I start to get pissed."

"He's sorry, Steve," Carl interrupted.

"No, I'm not." Keith laughed at the absurdity. "Look at the guy? Jesus. And you think I'm too pretty?" Keith addressed Adam.

"Mark's not on my client list," Adam replied calmly.

"Why the hell not?" Keith couldn't get enough of staring at him.

"Didn't we want to discuss what direction your career should take, Mr. O'Leary?" Adam chided.

"I want it to be gay, okay?" Keith hopped off the stool and stalked Mark. "Gay, proud, and out."

"Keith," Carl laughed as he called his name, "get back here and let's figure this out for real."

Jack shook his head. "Typical, Richfield. You walk into a room and all hell breaks loose. How many times have I witnessed this scenario?"

Keith leaned his hand on the wall next to Mark, admiring his height and licking his lips at his beauty. While he gazed at Mark, Keith said, "Steve, don't be greedy."

When Mark smiled at Keith with wicked intent, Keith went into meltdown. "Certain men really turn me on, Mark."

"Oh?" Mark batted his long dark lashes.

"Oh, yes."

"Do I have to get violent?" Steve asked in frustration.

"

He's only playing, Officer Miller," Mark shouted. "Just relax."

"Am I?" Keith touched a lock of Mark's hair.

"Keith," Carl kept laughing in amusement. "You're going to get hit. The cop is about to deck you."

Hating the fact that he couldn't taste this incredible man's lips, Keith turned around to see Steve's snarl. "At least you're nice looking. I'd be crushed if Mark was attached to some dog."

"You think that's buttering me up?" Steve pressed his fingers to his own chest. "Let's go, Mark."

"Go?" Mark blinked his eyes innocently. "I don't want to go."

"He doesn't want to go, Officer Miller," Keith teased.

"You're playing with fire, Keith," Adam warned.

"You don't mind?" Jack asked Carl in amazement.

"No." Carl sipped his fresh drink. "We've shared a man

together. It was great."

Mark spun around to look at Keith in surprise. "Share? Between the two of you?"

"Oh, *yes…*" Keith breathed hoarsely. "It was liberating. Ever have a three-way?"

"No." Mark smiled invitingly.

"Mark!" Steve growled. "Stop encouraging this!"

"Stevie! It's Keith O'Leary and Carl Bronson! How many opportunities does one get to have sex with the two hottest stars on cable television? Simultaneously!"

Steve grabbed Mark by the shirt and dragged him to the living room for a private chat. Keith turned around and gave Carl a grin, "I'm trying, lover."

"I see that. Good luck. I hope you win."

"Uh, boys?" Adam cleared his throat. "Why don't we just forget about Mark for a moment and get back to the problem of your careers?"

After Keith peered into the living room at the active debate, he moved to rest against Carl's legs as Carl sat on a high stool. Carl wrapped his arms around Keith's chest and placed his chin on Keith's shoulder.

"Right." Adam sighed and reminded them what they had been discussing before Mark showed up. "Your producers don't want any more planned straight outings. Correct?"

"Correct." Carl kissed Keith's hair.

"Okay. Well, I do get the reasons why." Adam sat on the chair Jack had moved closer to them. "They have a legitimate point. They are trying for a certain demographic and your pretending to be straight may taint that pool."

"So," Carl asked, "no more horrible double dating nightmares?"

"No. I guess not. But saying that. If you two come out, go hang out at gay clubs," Adam added with emphasis, "have three-way gay sex, and it becomes public? I really doubt I'll be able to get you another decent role, Keith. After *Forever Young* ends, you can kiss the movie career goodbye."

"Who cares? I'll do gay porn."

Carl laughed. "Yeah? You nearly passed out when you found out about the damn YouTube video. Who are you kidding?"

"Gay porn?" Jack laughed. "Really?"

Keith just shrugged, his eyes still on the doorway to the living room, wanting Mark to come into view.

Jack replied, "Adam, you should have Keith talk to Angel Loveday about doing erotic films. Keith will soon reconsider."

"Who's Angel Loveday?" Carl asked.

"An Eighties soft porn star that suffered a terrible stalking incident." Adam chewed on a pretzel. "Believe me, you wouldn't want to go through what that guy went through."

Mark suddenly yelled Steve's name.

Adam asked Jack, "You want to go see what's going on?"

"Mark's not my problem. No thanks." Jack finished his drink.

"See what you've started?" Carl rocked Keith in his arms.

"What's the big fricken' deal? One whole hour? Ooh!" Keith mocked. "It's like I'm stealing the guy's lover."

"Some men are into committed relationships," Jack said.

"And? So? Carl and I have one as well. It doesn't mean we can't have a little fun. We don't sneak around. We don't cheat. We agree on someone and enjoy him together."

"We don't usually intend on screwing the third party," Carl clarified. "He's just an accessory."

"Mark is so fucking hot!" Keith felt his cock become erect thinking about it. "I think their argument is ludicrous. It's not like we're asking for a year's commitment. It's one fucking time."

"Man, you sure make it sound logical." Adam laughed.

"Are you certain you're not a lawyer?" Jack joined in the laughter.

Mark's shout was heard very clearly. "I'll do what I bloody well please!"

Keith felt his heart pump wildly at the possibility.

"You do and we're through!" Steve roared back.

"You'd flamin' give me up just for one encounter? Give it a break, Steven! I'm not marrying the bloke!"

"You see what you did?" Carl chewed on Keith's ear. "You are such trouble."

"Some men are worth fighting for." Keith licked his lips. "Either of you ever seen Mark naked?"

"Not me!" Adam threw up his hands. "Ask his ex-roommate."

Keith spun around to Jack. "You lived with him?"

A pained expression washed over Jack's face. "Thanks a lot, Adam."

"Sorry. It was cruel of me. Never mind." Adam walked into the living room to check on Mark and Steve.

After Adam left the room, Keith whispered, "Jack? What's he look like naked? Big dick?"

Jack rubbed his face in agony. "You realize you will never get a chance at him."

"Why the hell not?" Keith shifted his weight to lean on Carl's legs more heavily.

"He and Steve are exclusive."

"There's no such thing for gay men."

Carl nibbled Keith's ear again. "Stop before you get us thrown out."

"Yes, I'm afraid there is." Jack smiled sadly. "If you'll excuse me?" Jack left the room.

When Carl and Keith were alone, Keith spun around in Carl's legs to face him. "What do you think of Mark?"

"He's very pretty. He looks like a woman."

"His face looks like a woman, but his body's all male. Holy shit. Did you see the bulge in his jeans?"

Carl chuckled softly. "I don't think his partner is keen."

"He's just jealous we didn't ask him." Keith leaned closer

and kissed Carl passionately. "I have the best fucking boyfriend in the state."

"You do." Carl dug his hands into Keith's hair.

"What do you think about what Adam said? No more dating those models? Sounds good to me."

"I can't stand going out and pretending like that. Forget it. Besides, you have any idea what Palmer was charging us for his services? We'd go broke."

"True." Keith cupped the back of Carl's head and kissed him again, tasting the salty pretzels and margarita.

Hearing someone step into the room, Carl parted from their kiss and looked up.

When Keith realized who it was he choked in awe. "Mark!"

"Hush. I'm supposedly coming in to say goodbye. Steve is going mad."

"Get over here." Keith grabbed him and dragged him so he was close enough to hug. Slipping his arm around Mark's waist, Keith inhaled him like he was intoxicating. "Meet with us."

"I really shouldn't." Mark expression said the opposite.

"Do you have a private line? Mobile phone?" Keith licked Mark's jaw, moaning at the taste of him.

"Christ," Carl whispered, "you are so fucking handsome, Mark."

"You'll swell my head." Mark blushed.

"Believe me, handsome, mine's already swollen." Keith forced Mark's hand to his crotch. Mark gasped and pulled back like he'd been burned.

"Mark!" Steve roared from the living room.

"One minute!" Mark shouted back. "Sheesh!"

"Number?" Keith ran his tongue over Mark's rough jaw.

"How good is your memory?" Mark hissed softly.

"Very good." Keith assured him.

"555-7132."

"Got it," Keith sealed the numbers into his brain. "When?"

Mark peered back at the door nervously. "Sunday around one in the afternoon. Steve has to go to his parents' house. He never takes me. They don't know about me."

"Date." Keith ran the tip of his tongue along Mark's lower lip.

Mark reacted as if he heard something, jumping away from their cuddle. He backed his way to the living room, staring at Keith and Carl as he did.

Keith licked his lips seductively at Mark before he disappeared. When he had, Keith wriggled against Carl. "I need to suck his cock."

"I need to screw his tight ass."

"Deal."

"Our business is done here." Carl hopped off the stool.

"It is." Keith couldn't hide his excitement.

When they emerged into the living room, Jack and Adam were whispering together. They stopped when Keith entered the room.

"We'll be heading out," Keith said. "Sorry if I stirred up any trouble."

"It's okay," Adam replied. "I think they worked it out."

"I'm so glad." Keith grinned.

"So? Did we get anything straight?" Adam asked.

"Yes. No more fake dates."

"Okay. I'll let Jeff know."

"Thanks, Adam. Nice meeting you, Jack." Keith shook Jack's hand.

He left the house with Carl, dancing as he did, thinking of having that androgynous male naked and willing to play.

Once they were in the car together, Keith moaned, "The idea of devouring that god has me so hot I can't stand it."

"Ditto." Carl backed out of Adam's driveway. "You remember his phone number?"

"Of course!" Keith laughed.

"I wish I had your damn memory."

Keith waited until Carl had shifted gears before he reached between Carl's legs. "Get me home. I'm in desperate need of your dick."

"Christ, me too. Maybe it was more than just Mark. Each one of those guys was hot."

"They were. But Mark? He was something else!" Keith squirmed.

"I don't see what the big deal is. It's not like we're going to see him regularly. I mean, if Steve wanted to play along, I wouldn't have objected." Carl downshifted and stopped at an intersection.

"He was just jealous we weren't fawning all over him."

"He must be used to people reacting that way to Mark."

"Doesn't mean he has to like it." Keith felt Carl's dick harden as they discussed the lovely Mr. Richfield. "I think it takes a real commitment to do what we do. Think about it, Carl. We don't argue about it."

"I suppose if Adam and Jack had the hots for you, I may get a little upset."

"That's the whole point, Carl. You'd come along for the ride."

"True."

"You think we should have asked Steve as well?"

"No." Carl hit the highway and accelerated. "I thought Steve was handsome, don't get me wrong. But Mark? Holy fuck. I've seriously never seen a man like him before. And Steve would monopolize him in a group situation. We'd barely get to touch the guy."

"Did you smell him? He was delicious."

"Oh, God. I am so horny." Carl checked his speedometer as he flew over eighty to get home.

"And we still have rehearsal all week and more lines to learn. We can't rest and play just yet."

"No. I know."

Keith reclined in the leather seat, massaging both of their crotches while he imagined another tantalizing three-way.

Chapter Nine

Carl gave his audition tape to an assistant as he waited for his turn to read from the script. Oddly enough, he wasn't nervous. Having the best show on cable TV to fall back on was quite a cushion. Every year they would renegotiate his contract and more money would roll in. Carl wasn't what he considered a materialistic man. He was frugal from years on a tight budget, including while living with his family back in Seattle. If he didn't get this movie role, there'd always be another.

The script wasn't one of the best he had read, and the computer graphics that were filling the big screens recently put him off.

"Mr. Bronson?"

He woke out of his daydream. "Yes?"

"Just a quick test for the camera."

"My pleasure." Carl moved to a masking tape X marked in front of a large camera lens.

"In your own time."

Carl nodded, looking down at the script with his lines highlighted. "You say it's a matter of time until the world is destroyed, Brad, but we should be able to do something."

The more he read, the worse he thought the script was. *What crap. You have to be kidding me*.

"We could use the ion blasters to destroy the satellites, but that still wouldn't stop Zorcon from blowing up the world."

After a few more pathetic lines, he lowered the paperwork and looked up.

"Tell us about yourself." The man's voice was deep and serious.

"I love pina coladas and walks in the rain," Carl teased.

A low laugh erupted from the small group watching him.

"How do you like your role on *Forever Young*?"

Here comes the fishing expedition. Carl glanced beyond the camera at the man who had asked the question. Mr. Casting Director. "I love it. What's not to love about a number one rated show?"

"Are you similar to your character Troy Wright?"

Here we go! Carl's smile faded. "In what way?"

"In any way."

"Yeah, we both drink coffee." Carl crossed his arms over his chest. *What's the fucking use? He didn't even like the stupid script.*

"Thank you, Mr. Bronson. We'll be in touch."

~

Keith reclined on the sofa, the latest episode in his hand hovering over his face as he committed the lines to memory. "More hot sex, Ms. Deavers? My oh my…won't the censors finally shut you down?"

The phone rang. Keith hoped it was Carl. When he realized it was his mobile phone, he tossed the script down and answered it. "Hello, Mom."

"Keith, why are you keeping your home address and phone number a secret from me?'

"Got a pen?" he sighed.

"Yes."

Keith gave her the information. "Okay?"

"Thank you. So. How are you and Jade Winslow doing?"

Keith groaned and fell back onto the couch, splayed out on his back, staring at the ceiling. "Ma…"

"She's very pretty."

"What did you want?"

"I wanted to talk to you. Does a mother need a reason to call her son?"

Keith didn't answer.

"I wondered if you and Jade would be interested in coming by for dinner sometime this weekend. Nadine, Harry, and the kids will be here and Nadine wants to see you. You do realize you and your sister hardly even speak now that you're a hot shot on TV."

"She could call. She has my mobile phone number." Keith ran his hand through his hair. "She never calls me."

"I'll give her your home number. She didn't want to call your mobile phone in case you were at rehearsals."

"Whatever," Keith sighed.

"Your father was so delighted to see you with that pretty lady, Keith. He had the idea you and Carl were, you know. I told him it was ridiculous. I even mentioned what you said during our last phone call. That gay contact disgusted you. He was very surprised after the argument you and he had in the restaurant. You know, tormenting him and telling him you liked touching Carl."

"Mom…change the damn subject."

"I will. It is horrible to speak of. So, what time will you and Jade be coming over this weekend? Sunday is better for us."

Thinking of Mark, Keith replied, "Sunday is no good. I'm busy."

"Saturday then?"

"No. Mom, while I'm involved with the show and the tight rehearsal schedule it's not going to happen. And Jade is busy as well. Er, she's in Paris now." Keith kept making it up as he went along. It was becoming too easy to lie. But that's what his mother wanted to hear. Lies.

"Oh, that's too bad, honey. When does the schedule lighten up?"

"Summer. There's a break in the schedule in summer. But saying that, I may be involved in a film during that break. I'm sorry but I'm just too busy." Keith heard the door and rolled over on the couch to see Carl when he came in.

"Too busy for even an hour or so? Keith, that sounds more like an excuse than a reality."

Keith yanked his zipper down and flipped his cock out of his briefs. "You can think whatever you want. I can't help it if the show is demanding."

Carl stepped in and smiled at him sweetly, instantly noticing his indecent exposure.

Just seeing Carl turned Keith into a sex fiend. His cock swelled instantly. Trying to tempt Carl over, Keith stroked it.

"I understand it's demanding, Keith. But neglecting your family…that's not right. Don't the producers understand you all have lives as well?"

"No. They don't give a crap." Keith stretched out as Carl approached him after tossing his car keys and paperwork on the kitchen table. "Mom again," Keith mouthed.

Carl nodded, kneeling beside Keith.

"That's terrible, honey. I feel very sorry for you that you can't spend five minutes with your mother and father."

As Carl's mouth enveloped him, Keith stifled a groan. "Well, that's life. Sorry, Mom."

"When you do get a free weekend, will you call?"

"You bet. Gotta go. I'm in the middle of memorizing the next episode."

"Speaking of that. Those scenes are getting really x-rated. How are you dealing with it?"

Feeling Carl's hard suction on his dick, Keith shivered and tensed his leg muscles. "Oh, I hate it, but I'm managing. There's nothing worse than having to touch Carl."

Carl laughed with his mouth full.

"You poor thing. You just do the best you can."

"I will, Mom. Just feel sorry for me."

"I do, baby. I do."

Closing his eyes as a flash of fire washed over him. Keith barely got out "Bye" before he howled in a sensuous moan. Tossing the phone onto the coffee table, Keith combed Carl's hair back from his forehead. "You give the best blowjob around, lover."

"Mmm..." Carl deepened the sucking.

"When you hum it vibrates my dick."

"Mmmmmm!"

"Ahh! Oh, Carl! You have any idea how much I love you?"

"Mmmmmm!"

Keith writhed on the sofa in ecstasy. "Let me take these off." Keith struggled to drop his jeans.

Still licking him, Carl helped Keith strip from the waist down. Once Keith's lower half was bare, he bent his knees and straddled wide. Carl crawled between his thighs and continued where he left off, this time, fondling Keith's balls.

"Ah. Better." Keith relaxed his back and reached for Carl's dark hair as he was serviced. Running his fingers through Carl's soft waves, Keith began to rise to a lovely climax. Carl tugged gently on his testicles, until he found his way to Keith's ass. Without penetrating, Carl massaged Keith under his balls, right up to his tight ring.

"Yes... Keep that up. Carl...I adore you." Keith felt the stirring become an unstoppable rushing of magma. Jerking his hips up, deeper into Carl's mouth, Keith gripped Carl's hair in both hands to hold him on target and shot come into him.

Carl swallowed him down, licking at the tip and pressing his fingers against the throbbing base of Keith's testicles. "You always need a blowjob when your mother's on the phone."

"Defiance. Rebellion." Keith caught his breath.

"I figured."

"How'd the audition go?"

"Okay." Carl wiped his mouth on the inside of Keith's thigh, continuing to toy with his stiff cock. "It's kind of a shitty movie."

"Oh? I thought Rossi said it sounded good."

"It's one of those high-tech computer generated types. I'm not so keen on those. I like good old fashioned stunt movies."

"Bet it pays well." Keith petted Carl's hair as his body began to soften and relax.

"Of course it does. I suppose that's the only reason to do it. If it's a bomb in the box office, it isn't going to boost my movie career." Carl fingered Keith's balls gently, staring at them.

"You can pass. You don't have to take it."

"They didn't make an offer. You know what they had the nerve to ask me? If I was like Troy Wright. Gee, what do you think they were implying?" Carl made a silly face.

"If you took it up the ass." With his index finger and thumb Keith tilted his cock to point at Carl.

Carl licked it. "Yup."

"What did you say?" Keith kept brushing the tip of his penis against Carl's lips.

"I said we both drink coffee," Carl laughed, sucking the head of Keith's cock in a tease.

"Good answer."

"It wasn't what they wanted to hear. Face it, Keith, they were asking me if I was gay."

"And are you?" Keith waved his rehardened cock in front of Carl's face.

"Nah. The thought disgusts me," Carl imitated Keith's words he'd said to his mother, sucking his dick again.

"I could have you do this all day." Keith angled his penis down so Carl could devour it.

"Don't we have lines to learn?" Carl lapped at Keith's length.

"I can read them, you can suck."

Laughing, Carl asked, "You really think that my lines will sink in with this gorgeous prick in front of my face?"

Keith ran it across Carl's lips again playfully. "Can't wait for Mark Richfield to suck it."

"Yeah, I can't stop thinking about that." Carl grinned wickedly.

"Let's turn him into a pin cushion." Keith's cock grew rigid.

"You mean?" Carl asked excitedly.

"Him on his knees, you fucking his ass, me fucking his mouth." Keith groaned in delight, "*Aaaaah…*"

"Yes. Can you imagine having that androgynous god as a sex slave? Getting us both off at once?"

"Ah, Carl…" Keith fisted his cock as he envisioned it.

"Come for me." Carl grew excited. "Jack off."

Keith licked his lips as Carl opened his own zipper, getting his cock out. "We're fucking sex fiends."

"I know." Carl stripped off his trousers. "Be back."

"I'll be here." Keith closed his eye, visualizing Mark playing submissive to the extreme.

Carl returned with the lube in his fist. He rocked Keith's legs back, exposing his ass, and slid his dick inside. "Oh, Keith."

Keith increased the speed of his hand watching Carl's face in elation. Bracing himself up on his arms, Carl thrust his hips against Keith's body.

"Come for me. Come for me, lover." Keith felt his body set for ejaculation number two.

"I'm there! I'm there!" Carl grunted as he came, arching his back and pushing in to the hilt.

Keith sprayed come over his chest, slowing his hand, gasping for breath.

As Carl recuperated, he chuckled, "Disgusting. Oh! Gay sex is so revolting."

Keith cracked up as Carl thrust in for one last plunge.

Chapter Ten

As Carl and Keith hurried to shower and get dressed for their work day, the phone rang. Carl gave Keith a quizzical look at the early hour of the caller. Keith shrugged, sipping his coffee and nibbling on toast.

"Hello?"

"Carl?"

"Cole. Hi. Are you calling to see how the audition went?"

"They withdrew the offer."

Even though Carl didn't really want the part, it stung. He dropped down to sit on a kitchen chair. "Did they say why?"

"No."

"Oh." Carl didn't even want to broach the topic with Cole. "Well, after the reading it, I thought it was pretty lame."

"It wasn't the best script, I agree, but it was breaking the ground into big films."

"Yes. I know. But I had images of it bombing in the box office and never getting another offer." Carl caught Keith's concerned expression.

To his surprise, Cole asked, "When is your next public appearance with Holly Lacey?"

Feeling his throat tightening up at the question, Carl didn't know what to say.

"Carl?"

"Yes. I'm here. Uh, Cole, the producers weren't happy about

that—"

"What?"

Carl could hear the anger in his voice. "They wanted our sexuality to remain ambiguous for the fans—"

"Carl!"

At his fury, Carl shut up. Keith was staring at him in agony, hearing half the conversation.

"Carl, listen to me," Cole sounded strained. "You forget about the producers. That's one damn show in what you and I are hoping is a long, lucrative career in the business. I'm advising you to go out again with Holly as soon as possible. This reversal from the studio for that action movie? It was an overt withdrawal in response to your sexual uncertainty. Believe me, they wouldn't have withdrawn the offer if you were engaged or married."

"Cole, you have any idea the position this is putting both me and Keith in? It's driving us crazy."

"I'm not concerned with Keith. I'm concerned with you. Don't you let that sleaze Adam Lewis affect our relationship, Carl. This is you and me. Client and agent. You got that? I can't make you and Keith get separate living arrangements, I know that, but I can advise you to be seen with a damn woman."

Carl was shocked at his tone. Cole had never raised his voice to him before.

"Carl. Answer me. Are you gay or straight?"

"I...I'm..." Carl connected to Keith's concerned gaze.

"It isn't a trick question, Carl."

"Why do you ask? That's unethical for you to ask me."

"I already got my answer."

"So? You're going to drop me?" Carl stood, unable to contain his anguish.

"No. But don't come crying to me when the offers vanish."

"Cole!"

"Goodbye, Carl."

The phone in his hand, a buzzing from the disconnected line

carrying in the silence, Carl looked up as Keith took it from him to hang up.

"You okay?"

"I'm in fucking shock, Keith."

"Come here." Keith embraced him, squeezing him tight. "Terminate your contract with him and go with Adam."

Holding onto Keith for dear life, Carl asked, "Why the hell does our sex life make so much of a difference to people? Keith, since you are the first man in my life, I was straight, pre-you. And never. I repeat, never, did anyone's sexual orientation matter to me one bit. I couldn't care less who they loved. Why does everyone care who we're with? How on earth does my sex life define me as a person?"

"It doesn't." Keith leaned back to see his eyes. "People are ignorant, Carl."

"But I feel as if I'm living in Victorian times. How far have we come to get away from the hate and ignorance?"

"Not far enough. We need to get going." Keith kissed his cheek and parted from their embrace.

"What am I missing here?" Carl felt dizzy.

"I wish I could answer your question, Carl." Keith handed him his car keys.

Babbling as he left the condo, Carl kept debating, "I need a label. What am I? Am I straight? Am I bi? Am I gay? Stick a tag on my forehead so everyone knows how to deal with me."

Keith closed the door behind them, cupping Carl's bottom to urge him to walk to the elevator.

"Who do you sleep with?" Carl kept ranting, "Well, if you sleep with him you can't act. Oh? You sleep with her? Here's the part. You can act."

"Stop torturing yourself." Keith tugged Carl into the elevator with him.

Carl dug his fists into his hair and growled in complete frustration. "You're right. I can't have Cole handling my career anymore."

"I'll call Adam." Keith took out his mobile phone. "How long is your contract?"

"Three years."

"We'll ask Jack how to break it. He'll figure out a way."

"Why? How would Jack know?" Carl exited the elevator walking to the underground garage.

"He's a lawyer."

"Oh. Good."

After they were on the road, Keith dialed. Carl was so angry and preoccupied, he felt as if he couldn't get focused enough to do his scenes at the studio. Things just kept falling on top of them. Carl couldn't understand why the fact that he and Keith were lovers had complicated their lives to such extreme. It was agony.

"Adam? Keith. Look, Carl's agent, Cole Rossi suddenly decided to go all homophobic on poor Carl."

Rubbing his jaw stubble, Carl felt sick. *I'm like some outcaste from society. Shunned by my own goddamn agent. And I'm paying that fucker?*

"Three years, Adam. Can't Jack break it for irreconcilable differences?"

"It's not a divorce, Keith."

Laughing, Keith said, "Adam just said the same thing."

Carl had to smile. Having Adam Lewis represent him was substantially better than Cole. Adam was supportive. Carl only hoped he never learned of their upcoming tryst with the scrumptious Mark Richfield.

Landmines. I'm laying the ground with landmines.

"Right. A copy of his contract. Yes. Oh? A statement of what he said? Really?" Keith cupped the phone. "Adam wants you to write a statement of your conversation this morning."

"I can barely remember it."

"I'll help you."

Carl glanced over at Keith, the man with the photographic

memory. It came in handy.

"Contract, statement…got it." Keith nodded. "Yes. He was really abusive, Adam. I only heard Carl's end but it sounded like he was forcing Carl to admit if he was gay or straight. I don't see what the hell difference it should make to Cole or the offers Carl gets. Adam? Aren't all the agents around here used to gay and bi clients? What's the deal?"

Carl showed his ID to the security guard at the studio gate. The man knew him by heart and always waved him through before he flashed it. Carl did it because it was the right thing to do. *I'm a decent human being. I don't commit crimes. I don't abuse anyone. I'm loving, conscientious. I give to charities, I support human rights. I'm not a vile creature to be treated like crap and denied parts I'm right for.*

"Thanks, Adam. Okay. We'll get it to you by tomorrow, FedEx or something. You want it home or at work?"

Carl parked and shut off the engine.

He had been so happy when Cole accepted him as his client. Carl remembered the celebration he had with his parents in Seattle. After so many rejections, Cole had taken a chance on him, an unknown. Carl moved to LA. He and Cole shared a bottle of champagne when he got the part on *Forever Young*. They popped the cork and Carl danced around the office. Cole kept assuring Carl he was going to be a big star. The producers and director of the brand new cable drama were top notch. The show was a guaranteed hit.

"You okay?"

Snapping out of his daydream, Carl took Keith's outstretched hand. "Yes. What did Adam say? Will he have me?"

"Are you joking?" Keith narrowed his eyes at him. "He just needs Jack to get you out of your contract."

"I have a feeling that will be easier than we think. Cole would be happy to see the back of me."

"That's my favorite view as well."

Seeing Keith's wicked smile, Carl pecked him quickly. "I love you."

"You too. Don't worry. Come on. We have a long day ahead of us."

Climbing out of the Vette, walking to their studio, Keith brushed against Carl's side. Carl knew it was for support. And he loved him for it.

~

"Boys?"

They had barely walked through the door when Charlotte flagged them down.

"I am so damn tired of this," Carl growled.

Keith touched his wrist to calm him.

"How are you this morning?"

"Fine." Keith waited. He knew there had to be more than that on her mind.

"Have you given any thought to our conversation?"

"Yes." Keith looked over at Carl. It appeared Carl was too worn out from earlier to deal with it. So Keith said, "We won't appear in public with Holly and Jade again."

Her face lit up as if he'd told her she'd won the lottery. She jumped and embraced them both. "I just love you guys! I knew the show meant a lot to you. Look…" She stepped back, reaching for both their hands. "I want to reward you. I know you're both antsy about your careers and the aftermath of *Forever Young*. Tell me…do you want to learn behind the scenes? Direct an episode?"

Carl perked up.

Keith didn't have the desire.

"Carl?" Charlotte asked.

"Yes!"

"Keith?"

"Uh. No, not really."

"What do you want?" Charlotte released Carl's hand and gripped Keith's in both of hers. "Tell me. More creative input? More dialogue?"

"More sex!" Keith announced wickedly. "Get dirty, Charlotte."

"More sex?" She laughed loudly. "I don't know how much more I can do without the censors closing us down."

"How about a three-way?"

"Keith…" Carl chided, but he was laughing as he did.

"Oh? Any star you have in mind?" Charlotte's eyes glimmered.

"He's not a star, but he should be one."

"Keith!" Carl choked on his gasp. "You're not thinking of Mark are you?"

"Mark?" Charlotte appeared to be a vulture on the scent of blood. "Mark who? Who's Mark?"

"Charlotte," Keith began, gripping her hands and swooning dramatically, "he is the most unbelievable fucker I have ever seen."

"Who's his agent?"

"He isn't an actor. He isn't represented."

"How can I get him then?"

"Keith, he'd never agree to it." Carl kept laughing.

"Wanna bet? The guy has a huge ego. Come on, Carl."

"Tell me. Tell me how to get him?" Charlotte rubbed her hands together.

"I'll talk to him. He's a good friend of Adam Lewis."

"Well, if Adam represents him, we'll give it a shot." Charlotte cupped Keith's cheeks. "You are so naughty! You've come a long way from the shy young man who couldn't even stand the idea of taking off his clothing for a shot."

"Charlotte," Carl sighed, "you have no idea. He's the exact opposite of that shy babe in the woods."

"Good! Good!" Her eyes were on fire. "Go to the set. We'll have a speed through first. Keith? When you get this Mark-god interested, tell me, and I'll see what we can do."

As she scurried off, Carl kept chuckling under his breath. "Steve is going to kill you."

"Why?" Keith walked with him to the set. "I bet Mark wants to do it."

"You really think that man is going to want to be involved in a sex orgy on this show?"

"Wouldn't you?" Keith asked in amazement.

Carl just shook his head, seemingly unable to wipe the smile from his face.

~

By late afternoon they had finished the speed through where the cast just read from their parts as Charlotte made notes. After the read they did the blocking. It was the same routine weekly, and by the next day they would already be doing camera and dress rehearsals. Weekly series meant speed. But Carl loved it. He didn't want to do anything else. That part in the action movie? It was crap. He was glad they pulled out. Sort of. In reality, he wished he could have been the one to say no.

"Carl?"

"Yes?" He snapped out of his thoughts.

"When you approach Dennis in this scene, think anger, betrayal."

"Okay." Carl winked at Keith as he waited nearby.

"Smack him hard. Get him to recoil and hit the bed. Then I want you to pin him back to it. You know."

"I do."

"Another slap?" Keith moaned playfully. "You know how hard he hits?"

G.A. Hauser

Charlotte laughed. "Would you rather have him spank your naked butt?"

Keith pointed at Carl in accusation, "You did that once! Remember? Totally unscripted while you pretended to screw me."

"I remember," Charlotte answered for Carl. "Did you like it, cutie?"

"I'm not getting my rump smacked on television."

Carl was having a hard time not laughing hysterically. Turning his back to them, covering his mouth, the recollection of spanking Keith on national TV was lighting Carl up.

"Oh, Carl?" Charlotte sang.

Forcing his expression to straighten out, Carl faced her. "Yes?"

"Slap his face or bottom. You choose."

"Oh, God!" Carl roared with laughter, doubling over and holding his stomach.

"Carl!" Keith choked in embarrassment. "My face!"

"His butt!" Carl was dying. "Please! Let me spank his ass."

"Okie dokie!" Charlotte gave Keith a smug glance.

"You're going to spank my bare ass?"

"God yes!" Carl dabbed at his teary eyes.

"I'm glad my father no longer watches this show." Obviously Carl's laughter was contagious because Charlotte was bursting with it and Keith couldn't help but join in.

Some of the cameramen and assistance were chuckling, trying to stifle their amusement as they overheard.

"I'll get you for this, Carl Bronson," Keith warned.

"Fine." Charlotte walked over to Carl. "When you enter the room instead of smacking him right off, toss him down on the bed and strip his slacks down. Then..." She shrugged. "I'd take him over your lap and have at it."

"People!" Keith's cheeks were beet red.

"Just don't get so wild you forget your dialogue. It is still a verbal fight between you two."

Controlling his hilarity, Carl kept dabbing at the corner of his eyes. "And from there? Just proceed into the love scene?"

"Yes. I would think that would be pretty easy after all that good discipline." Charlotte's eyes gleamed with demonic pleasure.

"No paddles!" Keith wagged his finger. "No leather straps. I know you, Charlotte. Once you get going…"

"Don't worry, Keith. I can't repeat that again. As they say, been there, done that." Charlotte walked out of the scene. "Give it a walk through. You don't have to bare Keith's gorgeous backside just yet."

Carl craned his finger at Keith. Hunched over from the embarrassment, Keith approached.

"You're the one who thinks gay porn is a snap," Carl warned. "So prove you can do it. Chicken."

"I'm not chicken. And this isn't a gay porno set. You see any fluffers?"

"What the hell's a fluffer?" Carl tilted his head.

"Tell ya later." Keith winked.

"Gentlemen? Any day now."

Carl inhaled a deep breath, trying to get into character. When he did, he spun around to glare at Keith.

"Don't look at me like that!" Keith shouted.

"Like what, Dennis?" Carl stalked him.

"Like you're going to kill me."

"You think you're funny? Humiliating me?" Carl grabbed Keith by the arm.

"I didn't mean to. You took it the wrong way, Troy."

Carl dragged Keith to the bed and sat down forcing Keith over his lap. The laughing fit was threatening to break free again.

"What are you doing?" Keith yelled.

Carl mimed tearing his slacks down his ass. "You deserve this." Biting his lip, Carl was about to break up with laughter.

"Troy! I didn't do it!"

Carl let go a slap to Keith's bottom. It was very light but still made Keith jump. He hit him again, imagining the sound when it was bare skin.

"Troy! Stop it!"

Carl couldn't hold it any longer. He started laughing, bending over to hide his face in Keith's butt. As he shook with it, Keith did as well and they couldn't stop.

Charlotte tried to get them to stop giggling, but her own was adding to the fire.

Smoothing his hand over Keith's wonderful bottom, Carl chuckled, "I cannot wait to do this."

In response, Keith wriggled on his lap.

"Christ, I just hope I can do it with a straight face."

"Let's go," Charlotte urged. "Pretend you got a few good slaps in. Go from there."

Carl nudged Keith off, mimed opening his own pants, grabbed Keith's hips and pretended to screw him from behind. "I'm the man in this relationship, sweetheart. Not you. Never forget that."

"Ah! Yes, Troy."

"You listen to my advice, Dennis. You hear me? It's the best for both of us."

"Yes! Yes, Troy. I know. I'm sorry."

Carl wrapped his arms around Keith's hips and raised Keith's body off the bed to meet his own closing his eyes and envisioning his dick deep inside Keith's ass. As he did, he unintentionally clutched Keith's crotch. Under Keith's pants he was rock hard. For a split second, Carl went wild from the excitement. Clenching his teeth, slowing his pulse down, Carl opened his eyes. Everyone behind the scenes was gaping at him in awe. Releasing his hold on Keith, Carl stepped back.

Keith spun around to say the last lines of the scene. "I love you. I know you're only looking out for us. I'm sorry, Troy."

"Well done! I can't wait to see it in the first camera rehearsal tomorrow."

Climbing off the bed, Keith whispered, "You okay?"

"Yeah." Carl struggled to slow his panting. "Christ, Keith, I just lost myself for a minute."

"Did you?" Keith purred. Twisting back to Charlotte, he shouted, "Are we done, boss?"

"See you tomorrow!" She waved, busy writing notes.

Keith hooked Carl at the elbow and led him out of the studio. "You hot fucker!" Keith hurried them to Carl's car. "What are you going to do when you're really slapping my bare ass?"

"Come?" Carl laughed, unlocking the car with his remote key fob.

As Carl ignited the engine, Keith tugged open the button on Carl's jeans.

"What are you doing? Keith, let me at least get off the studio lot."

Keith sat facing forward until they passed the gate. Once they did he twisted in his seat and unzipped Carl's pants, hunting for him.

Gulping the air, Carl tried to drive while Keith exposed his cock from his clothing. Splitting his attention between the road and Keith's head bobbing up and down on his lap, Carl was going nuts. The rushing to his loins was overwhelming. "I can't drive and come."

Keith didn't answer, speeding up his sucking, taking Carl down to his balls.

"I have to pull over." Carl searched for a good spot. "Oh, my God." Another first. A blowjob behind the wheel. It just kept getting better and better.

Carl pulled off the road and set the parking brake. Closing his eyes, he didn't care where they were. He was in Keith's mouth. That's all he cared about.

His legs stretched under the pedals, Carl couldn't believe how deep Keith was sucking. It felt as if all of him was being engulfed by that dexterous tongue and boiling hot mouth. Keith wrapped both his hands around the base of Carl's cock and squeezed in time with his drawing lips. Carl arched his body, pressing into the bucket seat and came, biting back his whimpering baying, like a hound yowling at the moon.

"Keith..." Carl battled for more oxygen into his labored lungs.

Sitting up, looking around, Keith cupped his hand over Carl's stiff blushing dick to hide it.

"I love you..." Carl choked up with emotion. "No one ever did to me the things you do. God, I love you so much."

Gazing out at the passing throng, Keith warned, "You better get soft, Carl. I can't tuck your big dick in if you're not."

Carl gently touched Keith under his jaw. The urge to kiss him was like pain. But they were exposed. The blowjob was a big risk as it was. Insanity. How could Carl prevent the devotion they felt? How?

As a tear ran down Carl's cheek at the injustice of their lives, Keith tucked him in and zipped him up.

"Home, James." Keith positioned himself correctly in the seat.

Carl placed the car in drive, released the brake, and merged back into traffic. The roller coaster of emotions he was dealing with was making him crazy.

Reaching for Keith's hand, Carl gripped it tight. When he could, he snuck a kiss at Keith's knuckles.

Hearing Keith's satisfied sigh, Carl began to grow resentful of all the ignorant bastards in the world. It was a personal affront. He took it to heart and grew irate.

Chapter Eleven

Keith slid a copy of Carl's contract into an envelope. They had worked on his statement last night and between the two of them, they remembered enough of Cole's ignorant comments to make a case of discrimination against him. It should allow Carl out of the contract. Carl thought Cole would be only too eager to dump him. But the man was still making money off each of Carl's paychecks. So it paid to do it right, with Jack Larsen behind them.

Keith licked the flap and sealed it. "We should FedEx it."

"Let's just drop it by Adam's office."

"On the way to work?"

Carl checked the time. "On the way home?"

Keith removed his cell phone as they headed to the car from their condo unit. "It's too early. No one's in his office."

"Leave a message."

"I could ring his mobile. He always answers that."

"Up to you." Carl exited the elevator.

"You're right. It is early. I'll leave him a message." Keith called the office number again. "Adam? Keith. We were thinking of dropping by your office to hand deliver the contract from Carl. Let us know how late you'll be there." He hung up, set the envelope behind the seat, and buckled up.

"Camera and dress rehearsal today."

Keith caught the glimmer in Carl's eye. "You want to spank me?"

"Why not?" Carl shrugged, waiting for the iron gate of the parking garage to roll back.

"I just never knew you had the urge. You know you can do it any time you want."

"No. Not really. I just think it'll be fun. I'm not really into it."

"You just want to tease me." Keith rubbed Carl's knee.

"You want to know why I really want to do it?"

"Tell me."

"All this talk and bravado about doing gay porn. I know you could never do it. You get so embarrassed by everything we do together on that set."

"It's not the same."

"How so?" Carl paused at a stop sign.

"By the look of the gay porn we saw at that club…"

"Yes?"

"It appears that there are several guys naked at the same time, all walking around with big woodies. So? Everyone on that set is used to it."

"You're sticking your dick into holes. And dicks are being stuck into you."

"And you get paid to boot!"

Carl laughed. "You are all talk."

Shrugging, Keith replied, "If it comes out we're gay and I get blacklisted? I'd do it. Ya gotta eat, Carl. And I'm sick of those pathetic commercials I did a year ago."

"Yeah, huh. Okay. We'll see how you do today getting your buttocks smacked."

"It isn't the same." Keith smiled, staring out the window.

~

"Good morning, boys."

Carl thought Charlotte seemed a lot happier now that they

agreed to stop seeing the models. The paparazzi had vanished as well, so Carl assumed they were yesterday's news.

"Hello, Ms. Deavers. Ready for another round of x-rated film?"

"X-rated? Please!" She waved her hand. "If I had my way, you wouldn't be pretending."

Keith pointed at her. "Porn."

"Yes! I'd love to direct gay porn." She mused. "But that's a man's world, I'm afraid."

"You are so dirty!" Carl laughed. "What does your husband think of all this?"

"He tolerates it. He calls me a gay man in a woman's body."

Keith choked up with laughter.

"You're a riot, Charlotte." Carl shook his head in awe at her.

"Go. Get into your outfits. Make sure Mel knows you'll be stripping Keith's pants down his bum. Make it easy."

Carl held Keith's arm and directed him to wardrobe. "She is so damn funny."

"I do adore her." Keith looked back over his shoulder.

Seeing Melvin sorting through clothing racks, Carl greeted him. "Hey, Mel."

"Hi, Carl."

"You have some Velcro slacks on there?"

"Velcro?" Melvin stared at him strangely.

"Yes. Rip away pants?" Carl started laughing. "I swear I won't be able to do this scene with a straight face."

Keith poked his finger into Carl's face. "You'd better! If you think I'm going to do this scene take after take so you can make my ass raw, you're insane."

"Whoa!" Mel gasped. "Make your ass raw? What am I missing?"

"I'll be spanking his tight butt. Charlotte wants you to make sure I can tug his slacks down from behind." Carl watched Melvin's expression.

"I have to see this."

"Here we go!" Keith threw up his hands. "Sideshow attraction."

"No. Practice for 'gay porn'." Carl laughed, kicking off his shoes.

"Gay porn?" Melvin choked.

"Don't listen to him. He's loony." Keith twirled his finger by his own head.

"You want to do gay porn, call Chi Chi LaRue." Melvin handed Carl his outfit.

"I'm joking." Keith slid his jeans down his legs.

"Who is Chi Chi LaRue?" Carl asked.

"Only the best damn gay porn director on the planet."

Carl gestured to Keith. "There. You have a name."

"Shut up," Keith laughed.

"Here. These are slightly worn at the button and zipper. Look." Melvin tugged at the ends and they opened quickly.

"Perfect." Carl started laughing as he stepped into his character's clothing.

"You're loving this," Keith accused.

"Duh!" Carl fastened his slacks. "By the way, Mr. Innocent, what did you tell Ms. Deavers when she asked for your input?"

"Carl! Hush!" Keith rolled his eyes at Mel.

"Enough said."

"That reminds me. Sunday, call M.R."

"M.R.?" Carl paused, thinking. "Oh! Yes."

Keith was hoping he didn't have to say Mark's name out loud with Mel there. Sliding on the pants, Keith tested the zipper. He barely touched them and they opened. "My luck they'll drop to my ankles during filming."

"Isn't that the idea?" Mel helped Carl button his shirt.

"No. Just during the big, fat wallop scene." Carl broke up with laughter.

"I'll give you a big fat one." Keith narrowed his eyes at his lover.

"Can't wait."

"Augh! I'm in heat! Cut it out you two!" Melvin started fanning himself. "Go! Get lost. Go see Ken for your make-up."

As Melvin hurried them along, Keith and Carl exchanged wicked grins. "You are so going to get it."

"Be careful," Keith warned, "payback is a bitch."

~

Standing on his spot on the set, Carl tried to compose himself. The last thing he wanted to do was laugh and break the scene. It only wasted time and he grew weary doing things again and again.

"Okay. Camera rehearsal. Ready guys?"

"Yes." Carl lost his silliness from earlier and tried to get into character.

"Bedroom fight scene. Camera rehearsal. Action!"

"Don't look at me like that!" Keith shouted.

"Like what, Dennis?" Carl closed in on Keith quickly.

"Like you're going to kill me."

"You think you're funny? Humiliating me?" Carl grabbed Keith by the arm.

"I didn't mean to. You took it the wrong way, Troy."

Carl dragged Keith to the bed and sat down, forcing Keith over his lap so Keith was lying over his thighs against the mattress.

"What are you doing?" Keith yelled.

Carl could feel Keith tense up in anticipation. Inhaling deeply, Carl slipped his fingers into Keith's slacks and briefs and tugged. He was stunned at how easy they were to peel off. Suddenly, Keith's fantastic ass was bare. "You deserve this." Carl grew erect at the sight.

"Troy! I didn't do it!"

Craving the touch, Carl let go a slap to Keith's bottom. The noise reverberated around the studio and made Keith jump and groan. It was so seductive, Carl licked his lips hungrily and slapped him again. Redness rose on Keith's bare skin. Carl was in heat and struggling to compose himself. They should have played like this together to get used to it. *What a turn on!*

"Troy! Stop it!"

After running his hand over Keith's heated flesh, Carl spanked him again, nice and hard.

"Ow!" Keith flinched.

"You hot mother fucker," Carl snarled, unscripted unable to prevent it from slipping over his tongue. Carl nudged Keith off his lap, stood behind him, and tore those loose slacks down Keith's legs. Once Keith's lower half was exposed, Carl unzipped his pants, knowing damn well he was hard as a rock from the foreplay. In order to hide it, he knelt down before he lowered his briefs. Once he was concealed between Keith's legs and against the bed, Carl grabbed Keith's hips and shoved his hard cock under Keith's body to keep it out of sight. Dripping with sweat from the excitement, Carl remembered his line. "I'm the man in this relationship, sweetheart. Not you. Never forget that."

"Ah! Yes, Troy."

"You listen to my advice, Dennis. You hear me? It's the best for both of us." Carl pumped his dick under Keith's body. If he kept it up, he could come. Just the sight of Keith's tight red ass was making him salivate.

"Yes! Yes, Troy. I know. I'm sorry."

Carl simulated a climax. It must have sounded authentic because Keith looked over his shoulder to see him. Pretending he had finished, Carl backed up, covering his crotch with the tail of his shirt. He stayed still knowing if he moved and the shirt gapped, he'd be exposed to the crew and camera.

"I love you. I know you're only looking out for us. I'm sorry,

Troy." Keith turned around on the bed, his back facing the cameras. When he did, Carl could see his erection.

"Cut!"

The assistant with the sheet raced over, concealing them. Carl drew up his clothing and wiped the dripping sweat from his face.

Once he was decent, Keith leaned against Carl. "You survive? I thought you were going to slip it in."

"I wanted to, believe me." Carl allowed Ken to mop his brow as Charlotte discussed different angles and lighting. "How's your ass? Did I hit you too hard?"

"No. Loved it."

Carl watched Ken's eyes dart to Keith. *Sure, Keith and I aren't gay lovers, sure. And I have a bridge in Brooklyn to sell you.*

"Nice one, boys!" Charlotte announced. "Once again."

"You calmer now?" Keith whispered.

"A little."

"The novelty will wear off. I assure you."

"Yes. I know." He smiled gratefully at Keith. After Keith gave Carl's arm an affectionate squeeze, he stood on his spot to start the scene again.

Carl took a deep breath. *I get paid for this! I get paid to smack my lover's ass and fuck him! Jesus, maybe those gay porn stars have the right idea.*

~

Two takes later and Keith's ass was raw. The last scene they had to tape in the late afternoon was dialogue only with Omar and Cheryl. By five Keith was worn out and very glad it was Friday.

The new episode in his hand, Keith followed Carl to the car, feeling a burning sensation on the skin of his butt. Sitting slowly in the low slung passenger seat of the Corvette, Keith exhaled a deep painful sigh as he settled in.

"I am so sorry." Carl started the car. "Keith. Let me take care of you when we get home."

"It's all right."

"No. Jesus. I ended up hitting you a dozen times."

"We have to stop by Adam's office." Keith reached for the envelope in the back seat and cringed.

Carl looked at him, a worried expression on his face. "I'm sorry. Oh God, I should have realized how many takes it would be and how many hits you'd endure."

"I said I'm okay." Keith rested the envelope on his lap.

"Let me run it in. You sit in the car."

"Fine." Keith didn't want to move. His skin was on fire.

"Where is it?"

Keith directed him to Adam's downtown office. After twenty minutes in rush hour, Carl parked in a crowded lot. "I'll be right back."

"Okay." Keith smiled. When Carl vanished, he moved stiffly, removing his seatbelt and tilting in the seat to get off his burning butt. "Holy shit. Good thing I have two days to recover." Running his hand along his aching bottom, Keith winced at the sting. Closing his eyes, he relived the scene. Carl stripping his slacks off and spanking him. Humiliating? Exhilarating?

Carl's dick was hard each time, and he slid it under Keith's body to hide it. But it felt so damn good under his own rigid dick. It would have been perfect if he hadn't had to do it three times. And Carl was so keyed up by the excitement he hit him hard. Keith knew Carl didn't mean to hurt him. It was passion. And Keith would have loved it, if...

If he didn't have to get hit over and over.

"Thank fuck it's Friday." A thought occurred to him. "Sunday. Sunday at one. Mark Richfield, I cannot wait to get my hands on you. Don't back out. Don't back out."

Keith peered at the entrance, waiting for Carl. He needed to get home and take off his tight jeans.

Noticing the script on the floor of the car, Keith picked it up, laid it on the driver's seat and flipped through it. Reading the italicized directions, Keith grew hard. "A three-way already? Wait. I have to ask Mark. Oh, Charlotte, how could you write it in so soon?" Keith bit his lip as he read the dialogue. "How on earth are you getting away with this?" *Censorship? What censorship?* Keith imagined as long as no one's actual penis was shown, and she did the sex scenes in fast MTV-style quick clips, she could simulate all sorts of sexual acts. "Ah, good old cable television." Keith heard the driver's door open. He grabbed the script and managed to sit upright.

"Oh, baby." Carl pouted in sympathy.

"I'm all right." Keith lied, clipping on his seatbelt. "What did Adam say?"

"He said he'd get Jack right on it."

"Cool."

"I'll be glad when I don't have to deal with Cole. At least Adam will legitimately try to get me good parts. Cole won't any longer."

"True."

"Aw, Keith. I feel so guilty. I never should have suggested to Charlotte I should spank you."

"Oh? You'd rather my face be this sore? No thanks."

"Let me get you home where I can rub some cream into it."

"That sounds nice." Keith tried to ease off his right side, the more tender of his two cheeks.

"Hang in there."

"Did Adam say anything else?"

"He did. He asked me if you'd dress up as a woman."

"What." Keith responded flatly.

"There's a romantic comedy that you're being considered for."

"Oh." Keith nodded.

"He said he'd find out more about it and send you the script. Something about staring with Ashton Kutcher and pretending to be his sister until you fall for his girl. A silly one."

"Oh."

"You in drag?" Carl laughed. "You'd be way too convincing as a woman."

"Shut up. I am not pretty," Keith argued, having been told he was too pretty by Adam nearly led to him refusing the part in *Forever Young.*

"You are, Keith."

"No. Mark Richfield is pretty. I look like a man."

"True. If you compare yourself to him…"

"Thank you." Keith tilted in the seat again. "Christ, why does LA have so much traffic?"

"Hang in there." Carl held his hand.

~

Coming through the door of their apartment, Carl tossed his keys and the script down and walked directly to the medicine cabinet in the bathroom. Scanning the salves and creams, he found some rich emollient moisturizer and hurried back to the living room.

Keith had kicked off his shoes and was lying face down on the sofa.

"Poor thing. Take off your pants."

"That's what got me into this mess." Keith worked on his zipper and dragged his jeans down his legs.

Carl sat on the floor next to him. Keith's bottom was still red. Squeezing out some cream on his hand, Carl smoothed the cooling lotion over Keith's burning flesh.

"Ahhh…" Keith moaned, loosening his tight muscles to sag into the cushions.

"That's it, baby. You relax."

"You're a bully."

"No, I'm not. I just get carried away by your looks." Carl massaged Keith's tush lovingly. "And your groans. Did you have to sound so sensual? Man. The noises you were making caused me to ooze come, lover."

"Mm," Keith moaned in pleasure, raising his ass off the sofa.

"Yes. Like that." Carl squeezed more lotion onto his hands. "Does it feel good?"

"Mm…" Keith humped the couch as if he was making love to it.

"You know this is what got you into trouble in the first place." Carl grew hard watching Keith's movements. "And you think Richfield is sex incarnate? Hello? Look in the mirror, hot stuff."

Keith faced Carl. "I should grow my hair like he has."

Capping the lotion, Carl set it on the coffee table and pushed a lock of long hair back from Keith's eyes. "It appears Adam is growing his as well. It seems Mark has a very strong influence on those who meet him."

"Why the heck isn't he an actor?"

"I don't know. Maybe he hasn't thought of that as a career direction before."

"Did you get what he does for a living?"

"No. We'll have to ask him that." Carl kissed Keith's butt cheek.

"Think he'll reconsider?"

"If you had a chance to have sex with us, would you do it?" Carl ran his hand over Keith's ass again, gently.

"Hell yeah."

Carl shrugged.

"Rub more cream on me."

"Sure." Carl grabbed the bottle. "I'm hungry. How about I order us something?"

"Yes, please." Keith closed his eyes.

As Carl squeezed another blob of cream on his palm, he asked, "Chinese or pizza?"

"Chinese."

"You got it." Carl massaged Keith's ass lovingly, knowing later that night, he'd be inside it.

Chapter Twelve

By Sunday afternoon Keith was feeling perfect and wondering if Mark was still interested. As the hour of one approached, he sat down on the sofa and dialed Mark's mobile phone number.

"Hullo?"

Keith was instantly turned on by his accent. "Hey."

"Oh, hullo, Keith."

"Are you alone?" Keith purred, imagining Mark naked.

"I am. Steve's at his mum and dad's for a barbeque."

"Still interested?" Keith found Carl listening as he filled a carafe for a fresh pot of coffee.

"I don't know. I really shouldn't. Steve would be very cross if he found out."

"How would he find out?" Keith wanted him. "You gorgeous stud. Come over here for some fun."

"You make it so tempting."

"Imagine it. Come on, Mark. You. Me. Carl?"

"You're both fantastic."

"And you get to play with us. Please?"

"You promise no one will find out? I can't lose Steve. I love him to bits."

"Cross my heart." Keith physically traced his index finger over his chest, though Mark couldn't see it. "This is our private affair. Just us."

"It's wrong. You know I know doing this is wrong."

"Mark," Keith hissed, "once in a lifetime. You snuggled between Troy and Dennis?"

"Oh...don't put it that way. I'll turn into putty."

"Mark," Keith breathed, "one hour. No one will know."

"Where do you live?"

Keith pumped his hand in triumph. He met Carl's eyes and winked.

~

Carl felt nervous. This wasn't an anonymous chauffeur. This was a friend of a friend, who was taken by a cop. A big, brawny, handsome ex-LAPD cop. *Playing with fire? Who, us?*

Racing around, Carl straightened up the condo as if Mark would scrutinize it for cleanliness. Carl checked his face in the mirror. He had just shaved and made sure he didn't miss a spot. Last thing Mark needed was a red face from a rough shadow.

The lube, the rubbers, everything they needed was on the nightstand. Carl lit one lamp, dimming the room by drawing the heavy curtains and blocking the outside light.

When he entered the living room, Keith was reclining crossways on the couch, his hand in his pants, diddling.

Carl checked his watch. "You think he chickened out?"

"Probably."

"How long will it take for him to get here?"

"Depends where he's coming from."

"Do you know that?"

"No."

The buzzer from the lobby sounded. Keith leapt off the couch like he was a gazelle. "Go!"

Carl ran to the panel, pushing the button to release the door latch. "He's here! He's fucking here."

"Yes!" Keith rubbed his own crotch in anticipation.

"What do you want to do?"

"Get him fucking naked!"

"The minute he walks in?"

"How much time do you think the guy has?"

"Yes. Yes." Carl moved to the door, opening it so he could see the elevator.

With Keith pressing up against his back, the two of them couldn't look more eager if they were kids waiting for the ice cream man.

Thinking that it was taking forever, Carl was about to comment on it when Mark emerged from the elevator.

"Holy shit." Carl melted to the floor.

Black muscle tee, tight black faded jeans, black canvas deck shoes with no socks, Mark was the picture out of a men's cologne ad, a gay jack-off magazine, *Playgirl*...all of the above.

Carl backed up to allow him in, slamming into Keith who was already wiping drool off his chin.

Once Mark was in their domain and Carl closed the door, he and Keith gawked at him in amazement.

"Hullo."

"Hi," Keith giggled nervously.

"Mark..." Carl shook his head in admiration.

Mark rubbed his hands together nervously. "What exactly are we going to do?"

Keith dove at him before Carl could even reply.

As Keith raised Mark's shirt up his torso, he backed Mark into their bedroom. "Get naked!" Keith ordered.

An anxious chuckle came from Mark. "No point beating around the bush?"

Carl stood back, holding his breath as Keith raised Mark's shirt up his body and over his head. Ripped. Perfect. There weren't enough words in the English language to describe Mark Richfield's body.

Following their progress to the bed, Carl felt his throat go dry and licked his lips as he stared in awe.

~

Keith was so ready for this he was primed. Dropping Mark's shirt on the carpet, Keith went for his jeans next.

"Oi? Am I the only one expected to get undressed here?" Mark laughed but Keith could tell he was nervous.

"Hell no." Keith stood back, yanking his t-shirt over his head and dropping his jeans and briefs to the floor. Instantly, he was at Mark's black denims again. Once he had them open, he peeled them back to see Mark's pelvis. Washboard flat with just the right spattering of hair. Yanking them over his hips, Keith found nothing underneath and almost spontaneously combusted from the sight. "Commando? Christ, Richfield, you know how to tease!" Keith spun around. "Carl! Get over here."

Mark reached back for something to brace himself on. He ended up against the wall near the bed.

Taking one look at Mark's fantastic face first, Keith began dragging the tight pants down Mark's large, muscular thighs.

Dark brown, curly pubic hair appeared. Keith knelt down, taking the jeans with him. Once they were at Mark's knees, Keith sat back on his heels to admire him. "Oh my God."

In reflex, Mark moved to cover himself at the ogling.

Keith held Mark's hands back. "Mark, you are unbelievable. Carl, have you ever seen a cock that big?"

Mark tried to cross his legs. "You're embarrassing the shite out of me."

"Oh, no way!" Keith chided. "Mark, you are absolutely fantastic." Reaching out, Keith smoothed his fingers over Mark's length. Mark moaned and his cock bobbed in response.

As Keith worshipped Mark's cock, Carl, now naked, wrapped

around Mark's neck and began kissing his throat and jaw.

"Ah!" Mark shivered. "Slowly, mates. I'm new at this game."

Yanking Mark's pants to his ankles, Keith helped him step out of his lower half of clothing until he was completely naked.

Blown away by his magnificence, Keith ran a hand up each of Mark's thighs to cradle his genitals. Above him, his partner was licking Mark's skin, moaning in pleasure.

Closing his eyes, Keith opened his lips and attempted to fit Mark's dick into his mouth. It was impossible to get it all the way in.

"Oh, love," Mark trembled. "Let me sit down before I fall down."

"Get on your knees," Carl hissed.

Keith felt his body explode with chills at Carl's words, remembering what they wanted to do.

"Me knees? Where? On the bed? On the floor?"

"The floor," Keith clarified.

Slowly Mark knelt down. "Now what?"

Walking around the bed to the nightstand, Keith retrieved the items they needed. Keith handed Carl a rubber, watching as Carl put it on his engorged cock. Keith had never seen it so ready. Or maybe he had.

"Is that for me?" Mark pointed to Carl's cock.

"I'd love to fuck you." Carl cupped Mark's face, kissing him. Mark appeared to swoon at his touch.

Keith pumped his own dick as he watched. It was better than porn. It was in the flesh.

"Yes, all right." Mark licked his lips.

Carl smiled wickedly at Keith as he moved, kneeling down behind Mark. Keith winked at his lover, and stood in front of Mark. "Will you suck me?"

Mark tilted around to look at Carl. "At the same time?"

"Uh huh." Keith ran his fingers through Mark's long hair and kissed him, shoving his tongue into Mark's mouth.

The whimper Mark made was worth his weight in gold.

"Yes." Mark closed his eyes and shivered visibly.

Carl checked with Keith. Keith gave him his most devilish grin.

As Carl prepared himself with lube, Mark reached out to hold Keith's hips. "We'll take care of you next, Mark. Promise." Keith petted his long hair lovingly.

"You'd better. I'm about to come just thinking about this."

Keith kissed Mark again, stood tall, and offered his cock.

Taking one last look at Carl as he moved to get inside him, Mark then opened his beautiful full lips and accepted Keith's cock.

The minute Keith penetrated Mark's mouth, he glanced at Carl. Carl obviously was in because he was thrusting his hips with purpose.

Watching Mark take it from both ends, Keith was already too far gone to hold back, but he did. He wanted this to last.

Staring down at Mark's face, seeing his brow furrow in pleasure, feeling him suck deep and hard, like he loved it, Keith didn't want to come. *Not yet. No!*

Mark's body jolted forward with each of Carl's driving thrusts as he went wild on Mark. Keith forced his eyes open to watch this incredible scene. The minute Mark stroked under Keith's balls, encouraging him to come, Keith did. He couldn't hold back if he tried.

Vocalizing his euphoria, Keith moaned in pleasure, trying not to collapse from the strength of the climax. He gripped Mark's shoulders tightly. As he shot what had to be a large amount of come into Mark's mouth, Mark whimpered in bliss, swallowing in quick gulps and sucking as hard as he could.

Behind Mark, Carl exploded, opening his lips and roaring like a wildcat in heat.

"Oh, God!" Keith cried as he watched his lover's reaction, shivering down to his toes. "Mark! Holy Christ!"

Even after Keith had come, Mark kept sucking, pressing Keith from behind to draw him in deeper. Keith watched Carl take few last deep thrusts before he pulled out to drop back on the carpet and gasp for air.

His body rocking with chills, Keith gazed down at this ultimate sex symbol.

Mark looked up at him with the most exquisite expression of nirvana. Keith dropped to his knees and planted his mouth on Mark's sucking the taste of his own come off Mark's tongue.

The brush of air against his body was the only indication Keith had that Carl had gone to wash up. When Carl returned he urged them both to get on the bed.

Lying back, Mark panted as if he'd run a marathon. His eyes were wild like a stallion in heat. His long, thick, brown hair was tousled and sticking to his sweat soaked skin, and his cock was enormous and protruding from him like an arced mast.

Keith dove onto his hips, lapping at Mark's erection as Carl devoured Mark's mouth and pinched his nipples.

Sucking as deep as he dared with a dick this large, Keith shoved his finger up Mark's slick back passage and worked his cock with determination.

"Ah! Ah!"

The sound from Mark was unbelievable. Mark's body rocked like it was about to launch. Keith prepared himself for the blast.

As come shot into his mouth, Keith moaned in delight, swallowing the nectar of this fantastic god down like honey.

~

Carl paused to see this fantastic man's face in orgasm. The sight of Mark in climax was beyond description. His teeth bared, his eyebrows knitted, his jaw muscles clenched. Carl grew hard again instantly. Seeing Keith lapping at that enormous dick, Carl lowered down to lick at it with him. There was plenty to share.

"Oh, Christ… Oh, Christ…" Mark gasped as he recuperated.

Keith whispered, "You ever experience anything like him?"

"Fuck no." Carl snaked his tongue around Mark's cock.

"More." Keith's eyes lit up.

When Carl smiled, Keith began sucking at Mark's balls while Carl licked at the last drop of come from Mark's tip.

"Oh, love…let me recover a moment." Mark reached out his hands. "Bloody hell."

Carl sat up to see Mark's face. Crawling up his long torso, Carl ran his tongue from Mark's sternum to his jaw. "You gorgeous mother-fucker. What right do you have to be so fucking beautiful?"

It made Mark laugh through his exhaustion. "I don't think I've come that hard before. Jesus." Mark held his chest.

Keith leaned up on his elbows, smoothing his fingers along Mark's stiff shaft. "Want to again?"

"In a moment." Mark propped up his head with his hand, his chest still rising and falling rapidly.

Keith edged up to be alongside Mark while Carl mirrored him on the other. Smoothing his fingers up and down Mark's flawless skin, Carl whispered, "Do you model?"

"No."

"Why the hell not?" Keith sniffed at Mark's armpit.

"I don't know. I reckon I never wanted that life."

"Do you want to act?" Keith nestled into the dark hair in Mark's pit, then began sucking on it.

"Not really." Mark gazed from one of them to the other. "Why?"

Keith rubbed at the wet spot he'd made under Mark's arm. "Our director wants us to do a three-way love scene."

"Oh?" Mark appeared amused. "That's a bit racy."

Carl ran his finger down Mark's abdomen to his pubic hair. "We want you to do it."

"Me?"

"Yes." Keith licked at Mark's pectoral muscle.

"I...I don't know. I'm not an actor. I don't have any credentials."

"You don't need credentials, doll. You have everything that's needed." Keith cupped Mark's balls.

"Don't you have to be a union member?" Mark asked.

"Technicalities." Carl sniffed Mark's skin, suddenly understanding why Keith began licking his pit. It was intoxicating.

"How...what type of scene. I mean, cable is not triple-x."

"No. It's not." Keith massaged Mark's balls enthusiastically. "It's all snippets, montages. Nothing really."

"Don't they do auditions for those parts?" Mark moved his hands towards his own cock as Keith began to make it hard again. Using his thumb, Mark wiped at the fresh drop that seeped out of the slit.

"We told the director about you. You don't need to audition." Carl sucked at Mark's armpit, lapping at him like he was dessert.

"What about Steve? He'd go completely mad."

"Why?" Keith ran his palm along Mark's cock. "It's only a small part. But it is a paying job."

"But telling him it's to perform a sex scene with the two of you? He'd never allow me to do it."

Carl leant up to be able to see Mark's face. "Allow you? What the hell does that mean? Don't you have a say in your own life?"

"Come on, chaps. Don't be so hard on me at the moment. I'm cheating on him as it is. And I love him. I shouldn't be here at all."

"What harm has it done, Mark?" Keith continued to stroke Mark's cock. "You're still in love with him. We don't want to break you two up. Carl and I are in love. We don't want another attachment. All this is is sex. Big deal."

"It's quite a big deal to Steve. He's very old fashioned that way."

"Then why are you here?" Carl asked resting his chin on Mark's chest.

Mark's green eyes darted from one man to the other. "I couldn't resist the offer. I've never been very strong. Ask Jack. He'll tell you how horrible I am."

Carl laughed. "Horrible?"

"Yes. I may look pretty, but I'm an emotional wreck."

"That's why we only want your body." Keith dragged his fist over Mark's cock, making him shiver.

"I'm terrible at making decisions. I've made a mess of my life enough as it is." Mark appeared to begin to back away.

"Stop getting yourself upset." Carl petted his hair softly. "See this for what it is. Not what it isn't."

"What is it?" Mark asked.

"It's an hour."

"I wish I could share that logic with my lover." Mark tried to sit up.

Carl allowed him, curling one of his legs under himself while Keith sat upright.

Once Mark was against the headboard, he pulled his hair back from his face and laced his fingers on his lap.

"How long can you stay?" Keith ran his hand over the soft hair of Mark's leg.

"Not much longer. I'm panicked he'll ring."

"What about the show?" Keith scooted closer still touching Mark's thigh. "Imagine being a part of *Forever Young*."

"It would be brilliant." Mark's eyes lit up.

"Come by next week. Meet the director." Carl knew Charlotte would eat Mark up.

"Should I? I shouldn't."

Carl could tell Mark wanted to. Who wouldn't? "Tell Steve you have a meeting. What do you do?"

"I work with Steve at an advertising firm."

"You work with him?" Keith asked.

"Yes. But our time together in the office is quite limited. We are out and about a fair bit."

"There you go." Carl leaned forward to nip at Mark's tiny nipple.

"I suppose I could at least speak to the director. What harm would that do?" Mark stared down at Carl as he licked his tiny erect nib.

Grinning as he lapped happily, Carl knew Mark was trying to convince himself.

Keith shimmied down the bed, burrowing his face into Mark's crotch with a sensuous groan.

"You two are starting me going again." Mark smiled. "Naughty, naughty."

A mobile ringtone sounded.

Mark froze. "Bollocks!" He scrambled off the bed and found his jeans. "Hush! Both of you!" he warned. Facing the bathroom, Mark said calmly, "Hullo, love."

Keith moved back against the pillows. Carl turned to look at Keith and then joined him as poor Mark suffered guilt.

"Doing? Not a lot. I was just out for a while taking a walk. It's so nice out. How's it going with Mum and Dad?"

Keith snuggled against Carl, resting his jaw on Carl's shoulder.

"Now? You are? Oh. All right. I'll just walk back to my car. Be a few. Cheers." Mark hung up. "I've got to go!" He picked up his jeans and was about to pull them on when he threw them down and sprinted to the bathroom.

Carl could hear the water running in the sink.

"He's going to smell like us." Keith sighed.

"Not if he washes well enough."

"I would smell you on him."

"Would you?"

"Yes. You smell divine."

"Not nearly as good as him. Jesus. When I saw you licking his pits I thought you were nuts until I went in for a sniff. Wow."

"I know. I could give him a tongue bath."

"Shite! Shite!" Mark appeared, scrambling to get his jeans on.

"Calm down." Carl stood up to hand him his shirt. "Mark, it won't help if you look like you're guilty as charged."

"No. No, you're right." He pulled his shirt over his head, tucking it in. "Do I still smell like you?"

Keith bounded off the bed and began inhaling Mark everywhere.

"No. I can't smell anything but soap." Carl held Mark steady as he slipped on his deck shoes.

"Right. Is that everything I came with?" Mark spun around.

"Do you usually go commando?" Keith asked.

"Yes. Don't worry about that. Right. I'm off."

They followed Mark to the door.

"Wait." Keith rushed to grab a pen. "Take our number. Call next week when you get the chance to come to the studio. We have to let the security at the gate know so they can let you in."

Mark took the paper, tucking it into his wallet. "A part in *Forever Young*?"

"Yup." Carl grinned.

"Too tempting to pass up." Mark grinned.

When he caught Mark's smile, Carl felt his insides burn with passion. "Thanks for sharing your body with us, Mark." Carl kissed his cheek.

"Yes. Ditto." Keith pecked the other one.

"My pleasure. Honest. If it weren't for Steve, I'd have truly enjoyed the hell out of it."

"Didn't you?" Carl gasped.

Mark winked playfully.

They watched as he waited for the elevator, Keith and Carl

were still naked and Carl hoped no one else walked down the hall. When he vanished, Carl shut the door and stared at Keith. "Was that like some weird dream or what?"

"Yes. A wet dream." Keith headed back to the bedroom and collapsed on the bed. "Mm I can still smell him."

Carl dove on the mattress and they snuffled around the sheets. When they came up laughing, they embraced and kissed each other.

"I love you," Keith cooed.

"I love you too. Thanks for getting Mark to come over. I really enjoyed it."

"Me too. Think he'll do the shoot?"

"I hope so. I just don't know how we're going to behave with that man in bed again."

Keith laughed and wrapped his legs around Carl's. "We won't!"

"Naughty! Naughty!" Carl teased, using a British accent.

"Get over here!" Keith rolled around the bed with him, sucking at his mouth.

Chapter Thirteen

Monday morning Keith led the way into the studio building. Seeing the group sipping coffee before they began, Keith smiled contentedly as he reminisced about the weekend's adventure.

"Hello, boys!"

"Hi, Charlotte." Keith waved.

"Morning, Ms. Deavers," Carl greeted.

After giving Carl a quick smile, Keith waved Charlotte over.

"Yes?" Her impish grin reflected theirs.

"We told our pretty boy about the three-way. How rude of you to rush us and put it into the next episode," Keith admonished playfully. "But he's interested. He's just worried about the union stuff. But you can handle all that for him, can't you?"

"I thought you said you can get Adam Lewis to represent him?"

Carl and Keith exchanged looks. Carl addressed Keith, "He'll tell Steve."

"Well, he'll tell Jack who will most likely tell Steve," Keith replied.

Charlotte waved them away impatiently. "When you have him here, let me know. I need to know by tomorrow."

"Tomorrow?" they shouted in unison.

"Let's go! Get to the set for our speed through."

When she walked away, Keith pulled out his mobile phone.

"What are you doing? You can't call him now." Carl looked past Keith to the crew gathering for their read.

"Hullo?"

"Mark?" Keith whispered, "Can you talk?"

"A bit. Be quick."

"You have to come here tomorrow if you want the part."

"Tomorrow? That's not much notice. I don't think I can persuade Steve in one night. I may have to pass, Keith."

"No. That's not an option. Let me talk to Steve."

"Are you joking?"

Keith bit his lip and knew he had to get going with their speed through of the script. "I have an idea. Tell me what time he leaves work and where he parks."

"What are you going to do?" Mark asked.

"Leave it to me."

"We commute together."

"Have him go first. Lag behind. Go take a shit. Anything to stay away. Just let me get to him alone."

Carl tilted his head at Keith in confusion as he listened to one side of the conversation.

"All right, love. But don't hold your breath."

~

Carl watched Keith nod and chew on his lip. He hadn't a clue what was going on.

"Black Mercedes...what's the plate?" Keith asked Mark over the phone.

"Keith, Charlotte's waving at us."

"Got it, Mark. Just don't be with him when he gets to his car. Tell him you'll meet him there." Keith hung up, stuffed his phone in his pocket and hurried to the set.

"Are you going to tell me what's going on?" Carl asked.

"Later."

Judging by the smirk on Keith's face, Carl knew it would be wicked.

"Are you boys ready?" Charlotte asked, the script in her hand.

"Yes." Keith stood next to her, crossing his arms over his chest.

"You need the script, Carl?" she asked.

"Nope."

"Oh? Keith bestowing on you the secrets to quick memorizing?"

"Yes," Carl laughed, "he's 'bestowing' on me."

"I'll bet." She squinted her eyes at him. "Fine. Let's begin. Betty, you have the first line."

Carl waited as the woman who played his on screen mother struggled to find the correct page in the paperwork. He adored her but it was an effort for her to memorize her lines. As he watched each actor speak or read their part, Carl's gaze came to rest on Keith. His lover had been staring at him. Keith's eyes were on fire with something he was planning inside his head. Carl could only imagine. But if it brought Mark Richfield into their bed once more, it was worth it.

~

After their day was complete Keith told Carl of his plan. "You want us to do what?" Carl choked in shock as they stood just outside the studio building in the bright sun.

"Shut up and follow me." Keith jogged to another door and opened it. A vast array of costumes filled the space. "Excuse me, I need some help." Keith flagged down an assistant.

Shaking his head in disbelief Carl had no idea how this was going to work, but knowing Keith, he'd succeed.

~

They huddled behind their car in the boiling sun, trying to hide. Keith elbowed Carl in the ribs. "There he is. Are you ready?"

Carl shook his head. "We're going to get in so much trouble."

"Follow my lead. Let's go. Wait. Put those reflective aviator sunglasses on. Let me fix your hat. There. Now I can't recognize you. How about me?"

Carl tugged the black brim of Keith's cap lower down his forehead. "This is insane."

"Oh! Hurry! He's almost at his car."

Carl sprinted behind Keith as he rushed to contact Steve.

"Mr. Miller!" Keith shouted in a deep voice.

Steve spun around, about to open his car door. "Yes?"

"We're with the police. Drop your briefcase. Put your hands on the vehicle." Keith pushed Steve to face his car.

"Police? Which department? Those aren't LAPD uniforms." Steve set his case down and placed his hands on the roof of his car. "What's the deal? Which department are you from?"

"Uh…" Keith glanced at Carl who shrugged. "Never mind that! Spread your legs!"

"Never mind that?" Steve scoffed. "Look, I used to be an LAPD cop and I have a right—"

Steve shut up the minute Keith reached his hands between his legs for his "pat down".

Seeing Keith nodding his head to join in, Carl went for Steve's suit jacket, opening the button and reaching for his chest.

"Ah, guys?" Steve asked softly. "Is this a joke? Because if it isn't—"

"No joke, Mr. Miller. We have some hard evidence that you violated the law." Keith mouthed, "Touch his cock!" to Carl.

"Hard evidence?" Steve laughed. "You don't sound very convincing as a cop. Who put you up to this?"

When Steve went to turn around, Carl stopped him, pushing on his back. Seeing Keith leaning against Steve's left side, Carl sandwiched Steve, pressing on his right. As Keith massaged the muscular ex-cop's torso, Carl dipped his hand into the front of Steve's trousers.

"Hey! Okay. I get the joke." Steve tried to stop Carl.

"No joke," Keith whispered seductively. "You are criminally gorgeous."

"I knew it," Steve laughed. "Did Mark set this up?"

Carl smoothed his hand down the front of Steve's zipper flap. A nice, hard cock was under it. Mission accomplished.

"Uh, guys. We're in the parking lot of my office." Steve scanned the area from over the car's roof.

"Do you wish we were somewhere private?" Keith purred, licking Steve's jaw.

"Holy crap." Steve shivered. "Do I know you?"

"Do you want to get to know us better?" Carl rubbed Steve's crotch and ass simultaneously.

"I...I..." Steve stammered.

"You what?" Keith sucked on Steve's neck, running his hands up his back and chest under Steve's sports jacket.

"I sort of live with a guy." Steve swallowed audibly, lowering his head to watch the hands that were all over him.

"Sort of?" Carl laughed.

"Christ, what are you doing to me?" Steve choked in a laugh that came out like a sob.

"What do you want us to do to you?" Carl purred, running his palm up and down Steve's hard shaft.

"Fuck me senseless. But I can't." Steve looked up with a start.

Carl and Keith winked and set back to see Mark standing

near the car, a big, satisfied grin on his face.

"Mark!" Steve took his hands off the roof of the car and backed away from Keith and Carl. "Did you set this up?"

"Set what up?" Mark walked to their side of the car. "Officers? Is there a problem?"

"Yes." Keith reached for Steve's crotch. "A very big one."

"All right." Steve swatted his hand down.

Carl took off his sunglasses. "Hello, Steve."

"Oh. I get it." Steve laughed, appearing relieved. "Hello, Carl. And I suppose your partner is Keith."

Mark leaned against Steve. "You get a woodie, Officer Miller?"

"Okay…" Steve smiled shyly. "Was this all-star performance so I'll let you play with Mark?"

"And you." Keith leaned against Steve's side.

"And me? And you're okay with this?" Steve asked Mark.

"Only if you are." Mark wriggled against Steve sensually.

After rubbing his face in his hands as if he were deciding, Steve sighed. "A four-way?"

"Oh yes!" Keith humped Steve's leg.

"Mark?" Steve appeared to be asking Mark's permission suddenly.

"Up to you, copper." Mark kissed his jaw.

"Up to me?" Steve gaped at the men in awe.

"Follow us." Keith licked Steve's cheek.

"Follow you?" Steve gasped in surprise. "You mean tonight? Like in no time to think this over?"

"What's to think about?" Carl took off his police cap to run his hands through his hair. "It's not grand larceny. It's just sex. Why does everyone seem to overrate that simple act?" Muttering out loud, Carl ranted, "Who do you have sex with? Oh? You can't have the part. What label is your sexuality? Are you gay? Bi? Straight? Well, we can't have you not have a label…"

"Okay," Keith pushed Carl to shut him up, "we know the schtick."

Steve gazed at Mark for a moment. "Do you want to do this?"

"It could be fun." Mark touched Steve's nose. "Do you want to do it?"

Steve glanced back at Keith, then Carl. "Fuck yeah."

Keith broke up with laughter.

"Follow us." Carl tapped Keith to walk back to their car.

"Okay," Mark replied, looking very excited.

As they returned to their car, Keith body-slammed Carl, making Carl push back to keep them walking in a straight line. "You did it." Carl stifled a loud laugh. "You smart son of a bitch, you did it!"

"Hee hee." Keith bit his lip on his outburst.

The minute they were inside the car, they roared with laughter, holding their stomachs and wiping their eyes.

"Keith O'Leary, you are amazing!" Carl started the car, seeing the Mercedes waiting.

"*Aaah*!" Keith kept gasping for breath. "How can Steve say no to the scene now?"

"He fucking can't!" Carl headed out of the parking garage.

"He fucking, damn well can't!" Keith relaxed in the seat and sighed. "We got Mark for our show."

"I am so impressed. You did it." Carl made sure Steve stayed behind them.

"An orgy with a sleek, foxy, androgynous model and a muscular, ex-LAPD cop. See? Fantasies do come true." Keith flipped the police cap onto the floor.

"Wouldn't our mothers be proud?"

"I know mine would."

"What do we do if there are photographers around?"

"They lost interest ever since we were seen with Holly and Jade. They don't give a shit about straight men." Keith ran his hand through his hair. "Steve still back there?"

Carl's eyes darted to the rear view. "Yup."

"Carl, let's come out. Let's stop hiding."

A shiver of doubt crept into Carl's stomach.

"Come on. Screw it. This is too much fun. Why should we pretend? They don't." Keith aimed his thumb at the car behind them. "Adam and Jack don't."

"We talked about this with Adam. Their jobs don't depend on public perception. Keith, remember what just happened to me with Cole?"

"Fuck Cole."

"No. Listen to me. Cole didn't even think I was gay when that casting director gave me the shove. Let's not come out like some announcement. We can just live our lives."

"You know that's bullshit. I bet soon the internet starts buzzing again with gay blogs. Then those piranhas will be back at our door."

"Keith, please. We're about to have an orgy and you're bringing me way down."

"Sorry." Keith grabbed Carl's hand. "You're right. Bad timing."

Carl checked the mirror again. The car was still there.

"How do you want to work this? We can't use Mark as a pin cushion again."

"Why not?" Carl asked.

"What about Steve? He's not going to let us do that to him."

"You don't know that. Maybe seeing Mark submissive gets him off. Let's just see."

"Christ, imagine all of us on him."

"He doesn't have that many holes!" Carl chuckled, pulling into their parking garage.

"We'll stuff two cocks in his mouth."

"Shut up." Carl laughed his head off.

~

They waited for Steve and Mark at the front lobby door. Carl leaned against the glass, gazing outside. Keith pressed behind him and looked over his shoulder. "All clear of vultures?"

"Yup." Carl exhaled a deep sigh.

"They'll be back. Once time passes and we don't appear with those women again, they'll catch on."

"Shut up. Stop talking about it. Look, there they are. Christ, the two of them in designer suits, couldn't you just cream?"

Keith pushed the elevator button as Carl opened the front lobby door. When Keith spun around, Steve and Mark were grinning like fiends. "This is so cool." Keith gave each of them a once over.

With all four of them in the elevator together, Keith felt exhilarated. He sucked on Carl's mouth hotly, peeking at the other two who watched.

Waiting for Carl to open the door to their unit, Keith couldn't stop staring at the men in silk suits.

"Come on in," Carl announced. "Anyone want a drink?"

Keith leapt onto Steve, wrapping his legs around his hips and sucking his mouth. *Drink? Who needs a drink? Isn't this intoxicating enough?*

Steve moaned, holding Keith's ass in his hand as he held him aloft.

"Holy shit," Carl breathed. "Mark, get over here!"

Keith opened one eye. Mark and Carl were kissing. Sliding off Steve's body to stand, Keith held his hand and led him to the bedroom. As he passed, Keith hooked Carl's belt loop and tugged him and Mark along.

Once everyone was loitering in the room, Keith wished Charlotte were there. They needed a damn director. Since Steve was the newest arrival, unbeknownst to Steve, Keith took special care in softening him up. "Undress, copper." Keith dragged Steve's suit jacket down his arms.

While Steve kicked off his shoes and unknotted his tie, Keith helped Steve get undressed. Keith was thrilled Steve was so willing and eager. There was no hesitation like there had been with Mark. Steve was pure confidence.

Undoing the buttons of Steve's stiff cotton dress shirt, Keith was pleasantly surprised at how buff he was. Tanned, swollen pectoral muscles, and a six-pack abdomen, prefect. Once Steve was down to his briefs, Keith stepped back to take his fake police uniform off. Turning on his heels he found Mark yanking down his Calvin Kleins and tugging off his socks. Carl was already nude.

"Jesus. Someone pinch me." Keith yanked off his clothing quickly. A hand made its way to Keith's bottom. He jumped when Steve complied with his request. "Bad cop!"

"Get over here, you pretty boy." Steve wrapped around Keith's waist, curling him against his body.

"I want this to be a group thing," Keith announced as Steve gnawed at his throat, sending chills over him. How could Keith explain he wanted them all to screw Mark? There was no doubt in Keith's mind Steve was an alpha male, and would be topping whomever he chose.

"Talk to me," Steve crooned. "You obviously have something in mind."

With Steve's hands wrapping around Keith's cock, Keith's mind was becoming blank.

"How about me getting on my knees or something?" Mark asked innocently.

"I adore you," Carl moaned, standing behind Mark, working his erect cock against the skin of Mark's hip.

"You want to play submissive, Mark?" Steve asked.

"You know it's what I love best." Mark crossed the room to Steve, rubbing his enormous dick against Keith, leaving a sticky trail of pre-come as he pressed against the two of them.

Keith shivered in a swoon. "Please tell me this is real."

Steve laughed softly. "Look at this cock," he whispered, holding Mark's in both hands. "Have you ever seen a prick like this in your life?"

Keith and Carl exchanged quick guilty glances. "No." Carl closed in on their group, reaching to touch Mark's anatomy.

As Mark arched back, shutting his eyes, three men were all over his genitals concurrently.

"Oh, bloody, bloody hell." Mark opened his lips and gasped.

Both Carl and Keith made a move to crouch down to suck it, laughing when they collided.

"Get on your hands and knees Mark," Steve commanded. Before Mark did, he connected to Steve's mouth first, hissing, "You know what I like, love."

"I do," Steve replied, his blue eyes sparkling in adoration.

"Tie me up?" Mark offered.

At the suggestion of Mark bound, Keith almost keeled over, grabbing Carl to steady himself. *Tie him up*? Keith pressed his own cock down as it ached for satisfaction.

"No, sweetie. We don't need to do that," Steve assured Mark. "You'll need to be able to use your hands."

"Ahh, Carl," Keith growled. "I feel like I need to jack off and come so I can hold out for this."

"You?" Carl stroked himself, reaching out to fondle Keith's cock as well.

"Get the rubbers." Keith nudged Carl.

As Mark dropped to his hands and knees, Keith flashed with the memory of him and Carl ravishing him. "I have to come. I can't stand this."

Just as he said it, Mark spun around and stuck out his tongue, licking Keith's dick. Instantly, Keith looked to see Steve's reaction. Steve's hand was out to Carl, asking for a rubber.

Carl tore one off the strip. Witnessing Steve's power and dominance in the bedroom blew Keith away. He wanted to come but at the same time he wanted to hold out. Keith had been in this exact position before with Mark.

"Carl," Keith called out to him. When Carl approached, Keith whispered, "Steve's going to fuck his lover. So you screw me."

"My pleasure." Carl removed a condom and rolled it on. The lube was passed between Carl and Steve.

Leaning over Mark to give Carl access to his ass, Keith didn't take his eyes from Steve preparing to enter his partner. It was so tender and loving Keith was in awe. He knew damn well that's the way he and Carl felt about each other.

"Ready, babe?" Steve stroked Mark's bottom.

"Oh, yes." Mark winked at Keith knowingly.

As Steve penetrated Mark, Carl did the same to Keith. Once they began thrusting, Mark slid Keith's cock into his mouth. Holding onto Mark for balance as Carl rocked behind him, Keith began to orgasm. He couldn't help it. The look on Steve's face as he screwed Mark was superb. Pure bliss. "Suck it!" Keith grunted as the sensation of pleasure started deep in his balls. "Suck it! Ah! Mark, suck it hard!"

That set Carl off. He jammed his cock deeper into Keith's ass and whimpered in ecstasy. Keith forced his eyes to stay open as Mark continued to suck him as he pumped his load, almost as if Mark wanted climax number two out of Keith. "Fuck Mark, Steve…" Keith urged, "Fuck him good…"

Steve gripped Mark around his hips and thrust forward, his back arching, his face a mask of orgasmic paradise.

As Carl dug deep into Keith's body for the aftershocks, Keith looked down at Mark, again, the last unsatisfied member. Who knew Mark loved it? *Tie him up?*

With the whimpering, gasping breaths of Steve and Carl still echoing in the room, Keith dug his hands into Mark's long hair as Mark continued to draw on him deeply, his eyes closed, lost to the world.

Steve sat back, taking a moment to recover. Carl pulled out as well.

When the two of them vanished into the bathroom, Keith stroked Mark's long hair away from his dewy forehead. "Get on the bed, you lovely thing."

Kneeling up, holding Keith's cock in both hands, Mark took one last, long, slow suck on him before he released him.

Helping Mark to his feet, Keith waited as Mark sprawled out. Mark's ribs rose and fell quickly with his gasping breaths.

"Enjoying it?"

"God, yes." Mark's green eyes flickered to Keith's.

Waiting for Steve and Carl to come back to devour this dish, Keith sat down next to Mark and ran his hand over Mark's silky skin.

When Steve returned he wasted no time. He planted himself beside Mark, cupped his face, and kissed him passionately. Mark moaned in delirium and gripped both of Steve's wrists.

Carl tapped Keith, pointing to Mark's cock.

While Carl lay between Mark's thighs, enveloping Mark's balls into his mouth, Keith knelt beside Mark and sucked his shaft.

Keith smiled. Steve knew. Steve knew damn well Mark was the main course to their three appetizers.

Mark began to give off those delicious moans of his. Keith imagined Steve's tongue down Mark's throat as Keith plunged Mark's organ as deep as he could take it. With Carl beside him, gnawing at Mark's testicles, Keith massaged Carl's shoulders and neck, loving sharing this with him.

Mark began to buck on the bed as he went wild. Steve parted

from his mouth so they both could breathe. When Mark's hands dug into Keith's hair, urging him to go deeper, Keith blinked and struggled to comply. Unable to meet Mark's body at the base of his dick, Keith was about to surround it with his hands when someone else beat him to it.

Keith's eyes sprung wide open. Steve was jerking Mark off with two hands as Carl was devouring Mark's testicles and Keith was keeping time with Steve's motion, throating Mark as far as he could.

"Ah! Ah! Oh, bloody Christ!"

At Mark's gasps, Keith prepared himself for the mother-load. It shot out of Mark with brute force and the quantity was awe inspiring. Closing his eyes and gulping him down as quickly as Mark could spurt it out, Keith moaned in pleasure. One of Steve's hands caressed Keith's face lovingly as if he knew the pleasure of tasting Mark's sweet nectar.

Keith was so hot once he had taken all of Mark's come into his mouth, he knelt up and jacked off over Mark. Carl, just realizing it, joined in.

The second orgasm was just as satisfying as the first. Well, maybe not. He wasn't in Mark's magic mouth. Spraying sperm all over Mark Richfield was intense. Hearing Carl's choking grunts beside him, Keith witnessed Carl's come adding to the creamy spatters on Mark's flawless bronze skin and dark, curly pubic hair.

While they pleasured themselves with the sight of his body, Mark recuperated, still panting for breath.

Leaning down, Keith began lapping the pooled come off of Mark.

It wasn't long before Carl was across from him, doing the same. When Keith looked up, Steve was kissing Mark again, more tenderly.

Once Mark was licked clean, Keith sat straight and stared at him, wiping his mouth with the back of his hand. Mark and Steve were snuggled together, sated smiles on their faces.

Keith and Carl lay on the fronts, resting on top of the men under them. When Keith caught Steve's contented eyes, he asked, "Nice?"

"Fantastic." Steve caressed Mark's hair as Mark rested, appearing totally spent.

"Uh, Steve," Keith began, sneaking a glimpse at Carl as Carl's cheek pressed against Steve's side as he relaxed.

"Yes?"

"Charlotte Deavers, the director of *Forever Young*?"

"Yes? I've heard of her." Steve kissed Mark's jaw affectionately.

"Well, Charlotte has this scene written for the next episode we're filming." Keith looked at Carl, pleading silently for some backup.

"And?" Steve nestled into the pillows.

Trying to be discreet, Keith kicked Carl.

"Hm?" Carl opened his eyes.

"Charlotte? The scene?" Keith prompted.

"Oh," Carl yawned, cuddling against Steve. "She wants a three-way and we suggested Mark. Okay?"

"Mark?" Steve asked.

Keith didn't think he should have been that blunt, but Carl seemed too tired to be tactful.

"Yes, love?" Mark asked sleepily.

"Do you want to be on *Forever Young*?" Steve caressed his hair.

"It may be amusing." Mark reached to hug Steve's arm to his chest.

"When does he have to let her know?"

"Soon." Keith felt his cock stir again as he kept being distracted by all the naked flesh.

"Tomorrow." Carl closed his eyes and burrowed into Steve.

"Mark?" Steve asked again.

"Would you mind?" Mark spoke lazily.

"No. Of course not." Steve kissed his cheek.

"All right then." Mark smiled happily.

When Carl's eyes blinked open, Keith gave him a wink.

Carl pursed his lips in a kiss.

Wrapping around Mark's body, Keith inhaled him deeply and closed his eyes to nap.

Chapter Fourteen

"Charlotte?"

Busy writing notes into the script, Charlotte took a moment before she glanced up. "Yes, Keith?" When she finished what she was doing, she raised her chin. Her eyes grew wide like bull's-eyes and she jumped to her feet. "Oh, my God!"

Carl gushed, "Isn't he gorgeous?"

"Do you model?"

Lowering his long dark lashes shyly, Mark replied, "No."

"Why the hell not!" Charlotte grabbed Mark's arm and drew him closer to inspect in the bright lights.

Keith leaned against Carl, his arms crossed proudly over his chest as their director admired the fantastic Mr. Richfield. "I think she approves," Keith kissed Carl's hair quickly after he whispered in his ear.

"Did you have any doubts?" Carl mirrored Keith's pose.

"How tall are you?" Charlotte never relinquished her grip on Mark's arm.

"Six one, two, something like that."

"Listen to him talk!" she stated enthusiastically. "I wasn't going to give him lines. He has to have lines." As if she couldn't decide what to do first, she urged Mark to a chair and sat him down, pulling hers up to his knees and staring at him.

"My God," Carl chuckled. "Poor Mark, he'll have to gnaw off an arm to get out of her sight."

"He's so bashful," Keith whispered. "Look at his red cheeks."

"You were the same way."

"No."

"Yes. You forget. Think back to episode one and two."

"How can I when we've done so many?" Keith met Mark's bright green eyes and smiled. "You okay, Mark?"

"Is she just going to stare at me?"

"She's thinking. Don't worry. She doesn't bite. At least we've never seen her bite."

"I bite." Charlotte informed them.

"Oh, my!" Mark laughed nervously.

"Right." Charlotte announced like she had an epiphany. "This is the scene now...now that I've seen him." She pointed at Mark. "I want you to enter the house with him, like it's written in the script, as if you're fresh from a club."

Keith's mouth was already watering.

"I want you two to undress him. Mark?"

"Yes," he kept chuckling nervously.

"You have any objections to being naked on camera?"

"Totally? Like in frontal?"

"No. Not frontal on film. We can't do that. But you will be baring your all for the camera and crew."

"Bloody hell..." Mark met Keith's eyes.

"I felt the same way," Keith assured him.

"What if I get wood? How embarrassing."

"You probably will." Charlotte smiled affectionately. "Still interested?"

Mark paused, fidgeting in his chair. "Right. Let me get this straight. They take off all my clothing?"

"Yes."

"Then what? I just stand there in the buff?"

"No. It'll be quick. Once all three of you undress you'll climb under the covers. It will be all of two seconds on show. Snippets. It's the only way I can do it and get away with it. The end result has to have the suggestion of what you are doing, without the reality. Do you understand?"

"Yes. I've seen the show. I know how you do it."

"It'll be the same. In reality, we'll show a quick back view of your lovely tush or chest and abdomen, and then you'll all be in bed."

"In bed…" Mark opened his hands as if to ask, "Then what?"

"In bed…" Charlotte's eyes grew wicked, "doing the dirty."

"Scripted?" Mark asked. "Do I have to learn some choreographed number?"

Keith cracked up. "Yes, Mark. Step one; put your dick in Carl's bottom. Step two; jerk me off."

"All right, Keith," Charlotte scolded. "No, Mark. With my sex scenes I try and let go. The actors know what I need and they take it from there. If I feel something is lacking I'll say so."

"So," Mark began, "they undress me. We all climb into bed. And we do what we feel like doing under the sheets? On camera?"

"Pretty much."

"Flamin' hell!"

"Want to be tied up?" Keith divulged.

Carl elbowed him. "Behave. This is hard enough for him."

"Will you do it?" Charlotte reached out to Mark's trembling hand.

As Mark chewed his lip in consideration, Keith moved to stand behind him and pulled his long hair back into a ponytail. He bent down to Mark's ear. "You get paid for playing with us in bed."

"On camera. I'll be in bed with two men on camera."

"That's what a threesome is, Mark," Keith reminded him.

"Yes, I know. I am aware of what I would be getting into. Will this be broadcast in the UK?"

Charlotte released Mark's hand. "It may get there eventually. Take a minute to digest it. Meanwhile, boys, we have to get a camera and dress rehearsal done. With or without the delectable, Mr. Richfield."

She left, giving them some time to discuss it. Carl sat in Charlotte's chair and ran his hands up both of Mark's long legs over his dress slacks. "What do you think, Mark?"

"I want to. Make no mistake. I'm just nervous."

Keith ran his fingers through Mark's silky hair, holding it in his fist, then shaking it out to fall onto Mark's shoulders and down his back. "We'll be with you to help you. Don't worry."

"Do you have family in the UK?" Carl asked, continuing to caress Mark's thighs.

"Yes. After the wedding fiasco with Sharon, my mum is staying in Hertfordshire with her family for the time being."

"Wedding fiasco?" Keith enquired.

"I told you I'm a horrible mess. You simply won't believe me."

"Forget that," Carl interrupted. "We have to make a decision here. Both Keith and I have to get going on a camera rehearsal."

"Yes. Right." Mark nodded in agreement. "I can't waiver. I came here to do it. And I shall."

Keith embraced him from behind. "I adore you."

"Likewise." Mark hugged Keith's arms tightly.

~

The crew was waiting impatiently. Charlotte turned around as they approached.

Carl released Mark's elbow, which he had been holding as they walked back to the set.

Mark smiled at Charlotte. "When do we start, boss?"

Her face lit up with fire. "You are fantastic! Okay, go get into costume, boys. Mr. Richfield already looks like a million bucks. Just take him to Ken for some touch ups and a good hair brushing."

"This way." Keith escorted Mark to the make-up area. "Ken?"

Ken spun around and his eyes grew wide.

"This is Mark. Charlotte wants you to get him ready for one of our scenes."

"My pleasure! Have a seat, Mark."

"See you in a minute." Carl waved at Mark and headed to wardrobe with Keith. "Do you believe this?"

"No." Keith started laughing.

"Hey, boys." Melvin pointed to the racks with their clothing already selected.

"Hello, Mel," Carl greeted him, changing into his character's clothing.

"Hey, Mel," Keith whispered conspiratorially.

"Yes?"

"Go check out the guy in make-up."

"Why?"

"Just go."

Melvin gave them each a strange look and left.

After he slipped on a pair of slacks, Carl zipped his fly. "What are you going to do to Mark once he's naked and in that bed?"

"Molest him?" Keith laughed, slipping on his leather shoes.

"No. Be nice."

"Carl, I won't be bad. I'm just kidding." Keith tucked in his cotton shirt. "I know how Mark feels. He's going to be petrified."

"Yes. He will be. We need to treat him very gently."

"I will. I was just joking." Keith turned around when he heard someone behind him. Smiling when he found Melvin fanning himself, he asked, "Well?"

"Who the hell is that?" Mel gaped.

"Our new sex partner in a threesome," Keith chuckled.

"You two are so lucky." Melvin fixed Carl's collar for him.

"You have no idea," Carl sighed.

When they returned to the set, Mark was waiting for them. Keith had never seen Mark look so handsome. His dark Perry Ellis business suit was tailor made for him. His crisp white shirt and dark tie made him seem to be a millionaire playboy. His long dark hair shimmered in the spotlights and his light green eyes appeared cat-like. He seemed calmer as if he had some time to reflect.

Keith reached for Mark's hand. "How are you doing?"

"Good. Better." Mark squeezed his fingers tightly.

Charlotte's commanding voice boomed loudly. "Okay! Start outside the door and come in. Keith, Carl, say your dialogue and get stripping as you urge Adonis here to the bedroom. I'd love it in one take, but if you can't get us through the living room and into the bedroom I'll be happy with the first half as one scene and we'll do another take."

Keith directed Mark just outside the model home's door.

"What do I say?" Mark whispered.

"Just moan and whimper a lot. If Charlotte wants you to have an actual line, she'll tell you." Carl caressed Mark's back warmly.

"Or," Keith suggested, "say what you feel. It usually works for us. We do occasionally adlib and Charlotte never cuts it from the scene."

"Yes. Right." Mark seemed to be concentrating.

"Okay. Let's go!" Charlotte roared.

"Three-way scene. Camera rehearsal. Take one!"

Carl opened the door and held Mark's hand as he entered the living room set. "I cannot wait to get you into bed."

Keith immediately began unraveling Mark's necktie. "Troy, I am really looking forward to this."

"Believe me, Dennis, not as much as I am." Carl removed Mark's suit jacket. "You beautiful creature," he purred, tossing the jacket on a chair.

Mark moaned softly, opening his arms as Keith unfastened

Mark's cufflink. Carl reached for the other wrist, doing the same after he unbuttoned the front. Mark's shirt slid off soundlessly and the sight of Mark's ripped torso put Keith into heat. The memories of making love to him and Steve ran through his brain like a favorite erotic film.

Carl kept edging them towards the bedroom where he and Keith knew Charlotte wanted them sooner rather than later.

Once they were beside the bed, Keith kept being drawn to stripping Mark when he knew he and Carl had to get naked as well. But removing Mark's clothing had become of paramount importance. Keith knelt down to slip off Mark's shoes and socks. He peered up at Mark to check and see how he was holding out. Mark's eyes were closed and his body seemed relaxed. Keith wondered if Mark was transporting himself back to their condo last night.

"I've never done anything like this before, Troy," Keith puffed out his line, growing very excited as an eager Carl unzipped Mark's slacks.

"None of us have." Carl parted the fine fabric of Mark's trousers and they dropped in a heap on the floor. Keith choked in shock, remembering Mark's penchant for going commando. Having no idea they'd strip him down to nothing that quickly, Keith heard a collective gasp from behind the camera and cupped Mark's cock to shield him. As if Carl realized their faux pas as well, he reached for Mark in the same way. Keith wrapped around Mark to cover him up, kissing his neck as he waited for Carl to get undressed in order to get Mark under the covers.

"Come here, gorgeous." Carl was finally naked and reached out for Mark.

Releasing Mark, watching him closely, Keith undressed as Carl brought the blankets up to cover Mark's lower half. It was something Keith hadn't expected to feel, guilt. He liked Mark too much to see him exploited. Suddenly, this little tryst left a bad taste in Keith's mouth.

After Keith kicked off his clothing, he joined the men in bed. Hugging Mark close, more for reassurance than sex, Keith kissed his cheek and neck affectionately as Carl mirrored him in his actions.

Mark finally opened his eyes, tilting towards Keith. Mark reached for him, cupping his head and kissing him. Keith moaned in delirium at the tenderness. Parting from his kiss, Mark turned to Carl, doing the same for him.

Keith felt so much remorse washing through him, he tightened his hold on Mark and buried his face in Mark's hair, struggling with an emotional wave that threatened.

"Cut!"

Carl muttered, "Oh, thank fuck," and lay back on the mattress to catch his breath.

Leaning up to see Mark's face, Keith gripped his angular jaw and cried, "I am so sorry we did this to you."

"What?" Mark appeared completely confused.

"Forgive us." Hot tears rolled down Keith's face.

The woman with the sheet held up to hide them stood by, waiting for them to get dressed.

"Keith, what do you think you did to me?" Mark brushed away the teardrops.

"Used you. Exploited your beauty."

"Silly man." Mark smiled. "I wouldn't have done it if I didn't want to. You act as though you tricked me."

"I feel like I did." Keith kept sobbing, the shame tearing him up. Behind Mark, Carl rolled to his side to cuddle, listening in.

"No. Keith. No. Please. Don't upset yourself. Yes, I am nervous. But I do want to do this."

"Mark," Keith whimpered, hugging him tight while Carl caressed Keith's hair.

"Everything all right in there?" Charlotte asked through the blind.

"Give us a moment," Carl shouted.

Feeling Mark's gentle kisses on his face, Keith knew some of his thoughts and actions regarding this man were not pure and wholesome. And he was filled with self-reproach.

"Forgive me."

Mark stroked Keith's hair back from his forehead. "What am I forgiving you for? I had two extraordinary nights with the two of you, and now you have me guest starring in the best damn cable drama on television."

"Naked." Keith tried to laugh but it came out a sob.

"Keith, love," Mark tried to get his attention, "you are not the first to become 'enamored' with my body. And I am not offended that you found it so compelling you wanted to keep enjoying it."

"Mark, at first I just thought of using you. I imagined you as some plaything. I am so sorry I ever felt that way. You aren't that way. You're sweet and kind. And I really feel like a jerk for ever thinking of you as anything else."

"Hello?" Charlotte exclaimed. "Show to do? Dress rehearsal?"

"Hang on, Charlotte, please!" Carl admonished.

"Don't be silly." Mark kissed Keith's wet cheek. "You didn't make me feel that way in the least. I felt adored, admired, flattered. You and Carl are the loveliest men. You think it was terrible for me to have made love to you?" Mark pecked Keith's lips again. "And the way you brought Steve in so I didn't have such horrible remorse over it was a stroke of brilliance. I don't feel as if I betrayed him any longer. That ate me alive, Keith. I love Steve with all my heart, and the thought that I had done something to hurt him was consuming me with shame. But you brought him into the act. And the guilty conscience I had vanished."

"Guys! Come on!" Charlotte yelled.

"Steve is a lucky, lucky guy," Keith confided.

"No. He's got his hands full with me. I would never call Steve lucky."

Keith climbed out of the bed and found his briefs. "You are very wrong, Mr. Richfield."

Charlotte poked her head behind the sheet. "This poor girl's arms are going numb. What's going on?"

"Nothing, Charlotte." Carl kept dressing.

Seeing Keith's tears suddenly, Charlotte hurried to talk to him. "Keith?"

"I'm fine. Sorry for the delay."

She looked behind her at Mark and Carl dressing, gripped Keith's arm, and drew him aside. "What happened?"

Taking a quick peek back at the other men, Keith whispered, "I just started to feel like we were using Mark unfairly."

"Why? Is he upset? What did he say?"

"No. He's fine. It's my own fault. I was treating him like an object and it was wrong."

A soft smile washed over Charlotte's expression. "Beauty is always objectified, Keith. Women have dealt with that for decades."

"It doesn't make it right."

"No. I agree. And if what we did made Mark uncomfortable in any way, we'd stop."

"He's okay. It's me, not him."

"You are sweet to think of him that way."

Keith didn't agree with that statement, knowing how much he wanted to turn Mark into a submissive sex slave.

"Wash your face and go see Ken for your eyes."

"Sorry, Charlotte."

"No problem. Scoot." She nudged him.

~

Carl waited as Keith disappeared and Charlotte returned. "Is Keith okay?"

"He's fine. I just need his face fixed. Okay." She grinned at Mark as he tied his necktie. "You need a line. Though you look scrumptious just standing there, it seems unnatural for you to not say a word."

"What should I say?" Mark tightened the knot under his chin.

Reaching up to assist, Charlotte straightened it for him. "Tell them how much you have always wanted to do it as well. Perhaps after Carl says 'You beautiful creature', you say 'You don't know how long I've waited to make love to two men.' Something like that."

"All right." Mark smiled.

Charlotte cupped his face and shouted, "Gorgeous! Gorgeous!" in excitement as she rushed off the set.

"She's a little dynamo," Mark whispered to Carl.

"A little pervo more like it." Carl shook his head.

Seeing Keith returning, Carl hurried over to him. "You okay, babe?"

"Yes. How's Mark?"

Hearing him, Mark replied softly. "I'm fine. Better now that I know what to expect."

"The first time is the worst. It does get easier." Carl urged them outside the set door again in preparation for their scene.

"Mark," Keith whispered, "turn your back to the cameras."

"Yes. I shall."

"Carl, let's undress him that way. There's no need for the crew to keep getting an eye-full."

"I agree." Carl rubbed Mark's back warmly in a comforting gesture.

"Ready, gentlemen?" Charlotte boomed.

"Yes, Mother!" Carl replied.

"Threesome scene. Take one. Action!"

In a silent hiss, Carl asked, "Ready, boys?" and he swung open the door, escorting Mark into the living room. "I cannot wait to get you into bed." Carl could feel Mark wasn't nearly as nervous as before.

Turning Mark so his back was to the cameras, Keith began unraveling Mark's necktie. "Troy, I am really looking forward to this."

"Believe me, Dennis, not as much as I am." Once again Carl removed Mark's suit jacket. "You beautiful creature." Carl smiled at Mark adoringly, tossing the jacket on a chair.

Mark moaned softly, "Yes, this is my first time as well. I've always wondered what making love to two men would be like."

Carl was so proud of Mark. It took balls to act on camera, especially with no training that Carl knew of.

This time Mark helped Keith as he unfastened Mark's cufflink. Liking the way it worked last time, Carl reached for Mark's other wrist, doing the same. Mark removed his shirt, setting it with his jacket on a chair.

It was easier with Mark undressing himself. Carl was able to start on his own clothing. Tapping Keith, he urged them to the bedroom. The clothing was coming off much faster this take. And when Mark's trousers dropped, he only revealed a back view to the hungry cameras and crew.

"I've never done anything like this before, Troy," Keith said his line, standing next to Mark, facing the back wall. Keith smoothed his hand over Mark's shoulder.

"None of us have." Carl turned down the bed, climbing in, holding up the sheets to assist Mark in joining him.

"Come here, gorgeous." Carl wrapped around Mark to give him a big hug.

Keith embraced Mark as well, kissing his cheek and neck affectionately as Carl did the same.

"Oh, I'm in heaven," Mark moaned, wriggling between them.

"So are we, beautiful, so are we," Keith sighed, tilting Mark's jaw in his direction and kissing him.

"Cut!"

"Nicely done, boys! I don't see how we could improve on

that one."

Keith wrapped his legs and arms tighter around Mark. "Thank you for being such a good sport, Mark."

"Are you joking? I loved it."

"Christ, you always smell so good." Carl snuffled Mark hungrily.

The woman with the sheet waited, her arms extended towards the ceiling, yet no one was getting out of the bed.

Charlotte peeked in. "Still okay?"

Purring, writhing against Mark, Keith smiled. "We don't want to get out."

"I'd sell my soul to climb in there with you three."

"Charlotte!" Carl choked in shock, breaking up with laughter.

Mark craned his finger at her. "Come on in, sweetie."

"Augh! Don't you dare!" She turned beet red. Keith was astonished. He didn't think the brazen Charlotte Deavers could blush at anything.

Keith's dick went rigid at Mark's playful teasing. Unable to control himself, he licked Mark's cheek, leaving a wet trail up his jaw. Mark twisted around and kissed him passionately.

"Augh! Drop the sheets! Roll! Roll!" Charlotte raced out of the scene, dragging the assistant with the blind with her.

Lost on Mark's tongue, Keith felt Carl's hands finding their way between he and Mark, clamping both their erections together. Keith shivered and reached around Mark to touch his lover. When he felt Carl's mouth sucking his middle finger Keith went wild. "We can't do this. We're on film," he breathed as quietly as he could.

"Film? What film?" Mark teased as he rolled on top of Keith and spread his legs.

"Oh, holy shit," Carl moaned. "Guys, we can't do this. They are taping."

Mark leaned up on his elbows and turned to look at the crew. When he did, Keith propped up his head to see what Mark saw.

Four cameras, twenty assistants, and Charlotte, all gawking.

"No. Carl's quite right. We'll regret this," Mark agreed.

"Charlotte, cut!" Carl ordered.

"Cut! Cut." She sighed. "Damn. We really had something special there for a minute, Carl."

"When does it stop being a public display and get personal?" Mark asked innocently, sitting up with the blanket around his hips.

"Good question." Keith leaned back against the headboard.

"This better not show up on YouTube." Carl appeared to be searching the crew carefully.

"Get up." Keith panicked at the notion. "Sheet!"

The woman with the blind raced over.

"Get dressed," Keith prodded Mark.

Mark quickly got out of the bed and found his trousers. "YouTube? What's that about? Should I be nervous?"

"No. Carl, stop freaking us out." Keith zipped his fly. "If it shows up on the net we claim it's the shoot. We can't help what they write for us."

"I know that. But does the public know that?"

"What's all this? You didn't mention anything going on the Internet." Mark buttoned his shirt.

"It won't. Carl, stop it." Keith felt sick to have placed Mark in that predicament. The guilt just wouldn't end.

"Does the studio do that?" Mark asked. "You know, coming attractions? Trailers?"

"That's not what Carl is referring to. Never mind, Mark. There's no sense getting upset about something that might not happen." Keith slipped his shoes on.

"Won't it?" Carl narrowed his eyes at Keith.

The woman with the sheet walked away once they were all decent. Carl helped Mark with his cufflinks as Charlotte approached him. "Mark, we need all your information for your paycheck and the tax man."

"Yes. Of course." Mark nodded, thanking Carl for his help.

"And Adam Lewis is your agent?" she asked.

Mark exchanged glances with Keith and Carl. "I suppose Jack will find out when he watches the show."

"Jack?" Charlotte asked.

"Never mind. Yes," Keith said, "Adam is Mark's agent."

"Good. It's been an absolute delight getting to work with you, Mark. I'll keep you in mind for my next series. And...there's always a chance you may return for a guest spot."

"Great. Cheers." Mark shook her hand. When she walked away, Mark checked his watch. "I should get to the office."

"Thanks again, Mark." Keith hugged him.

"My pleasure. You just remember that." Mark caressed Keith's face.

"See you soon?" Carl reached out his hand.

Mark took it. "I do hope so. You should come round to Jack and Adam's place when we have pizza night and show Loveday videos."

"Loveday again?" Keith puzzled. "Who the heck is this Loveday guy you all keep mentioning."

"If you don't know," Mark grinned wickedly, "you ought to find out. Come by and you'll see what all the fuss is about."

"We will," Carl agreed, waving as Mark left.

Once he vanished, Charlotte yelled for them to come back and do the next scene. As they did, Keith sighed, "That was a very weird experience."

"What isn't weird in show business?" Carl walked with Keith back to the set.

Chapter Fifteen

Keith was completely spent by the time they arrived home from the studio. Scuffing his feet wearily, he followed Carl into their condo and kicked off his shoes, falling back on the sofa with a groan.

"What a day." Carl tossed his keys on the counter. "I'm beat."

"Me too. I had no idea that scene with Mark would take it out of me. I thought it would be another fun romp. It was and it wasn't."

Removing his shoes and socks to get comfy in the warm room, Carl raised Keith's legs, collapsed under them on the cushion, resting them across his lap. "You really felt bad about Mark, didn't you?"

"Yes. Come on, Carl. We used him."

"He liked it. He even wanted to play submissive." Carl tugged off Keith's socks, massaging his feet.

"Justify it any way you like. I still feel like crap about it."

"Even with Mark's reassurances?"

"The guy's too innocent for his own good. He doesn't even know when he's being objectified." Keith closed his eyes. "That feels excellent."

Carl pushed Keith's jeans up his shins, rubbing his ankles and digging under the fabric to his calves. "I think the three-way, and for that matter, the group thing, is over for us."

"I agree. It was a thrill, but we've done it. I imagine if we make a habit of it, even that will wear on us."

"I love you. You and I think so much alike."

Opening his eyes, Keith smiled adoringly at him. "It was nice to do things like that together. Share the experiences."

"Definitely. It brought us closer."

"It did, Carl. It definitely did."

"I know."

"Marry me."

Choking on a laugh, Carl asked, "What?"

"Marry me. It's legal here now."

"Keith..." Carl fixed Keith's pant legs, covering his shins again.

"We can do it secretly."

"Then what's the point?"

"Huh?" Keith reached for Carl's hand.

"I said, what's the point of a secret ceremony? If we can't celebrate it with family and friends, why do it?"

"You want to have a big wedding?"

Appearing frustrated, Carl rested his head on the back of the couch, staring at the ceiling. "We can't get married, Keith."

"Carl..." Keith placed his feet on the floor and cuddled against Carl's side. "I love you. I don't want anyone else but you."

"Our careers, Keith. Remember Adam? Deny, deny, deny? How do we deny we're a couple if we get married?"

Keith wrapped around Carl and dragged him down on top of him lengthwise on the sofa. He then clasped both of Carl's hands and crushed them to his chest. "How long do you want to play this stupid game, Carl?"

"As long as we both have careers in acting, Keith."

"No. No way."

"Keith, I want to star in movies. And not as the cartoonish fag who lisps and waves his hands around like a queen."

Winding his legs around Carl's, Keith moaned, "Carl...please."

Pulling away just enough to talk to him, Carl leaned his elbows on the arm of the couch over Keith's head and spoke in a serious tone, "I love you, I do. This has got nothing to do with the amount I adore you and want you with me. The answer to that is forever."

"Like in *Forever Young*?" Keith sneered sarcastically.

"Don't be glib. You know what I'm talking about here."

Dropping one foot to the floor, Keith stamped it in frustration.

Carl leaned down and kissed Keith's lips. "I'm sorry, Keith. I want a career."

"In secret. A tiny little ceremony with Adam, Jack, Mark, and Steve."

"Secret? In Hollywood? Are you joking?"

"No one will know."

"What about wedding rings?" Carl asked, accusing. "Huh, Keith? We suddenly wear rings?"

"No rings."

Carl sat up, pushing away from Keith. "Then what's the fucking point? Who are we kidding?"

"Please don't pull away from me."

Crossing his arms over his chest in anger, Carl shook his head.

"Do you love me?"

"You know I do."

"Will you do anything for me?"

Carl peered over at him. The green of Carl's irises were paler than Mark's and had a gold ring around the outer edge. Mesmerizing.

"Almost."

"Almost anything?"

"Yes. That's what I said."

Sitting up again to be able to whisper, Keith asked, "You'll do anything I ask sexually, but you won't have a commitment ceremony with me. Don't you think that's unfair?"

"I didn't make the rules. Society did."

"And since when do we give a shit what 'society' thinks?"

"I can't keep going over this with you." Carl stood abruptly. "I'm taking a shower."

When Carl left the room, Keith slumped over his lap rubbing his face in agony. He loved Carl. Why did it matter to anyone?

The phone rang. It scared the crap out of Keith he was so deep in thought. He hopped up and picked up the cordless. "Hello?"

"Keith. Charlotte."

"Hi. What's up?"

"Are you sitting down?"

"Should I be?" Keith flopped to the couch.

"Yes."

"I'm sitting."

"Is Carl with you?"

"He's in the shower. What's going on, Charlotte?"

"You and he both have been nominated for Emmys."

"Have we? Derek Dixon and Will Markham hinted about it when they spoke to us about the women. Do you know that for sure?"

"Yes. I just got a phone call from a trusted source, Keith. The show has got six nominations."

"Wow. Cool."

"Will you two go together? You know, as a couple?"

"Oh, God. Charlotte." Keith felt sick, rubbing his eyes tiredly.

"Please don't go with those toothpicks. You promised me, Derek, and Will that was finished."

"Toothpicks?" Keith asked. "You mean Holly and Jade? They're not toothpicks, Charlotte. They're women."

"Barely."

"Come on, I don't need this."

"No. You should be popping the champagne corks."

"Yeah. Whoopee."

"Keith!"

"Sorry. Yes. It's great, Charlotte. I do appreciate the call."

"Please don't worry about coming with Carl. People expect it."

"No. They don't. But nice try."

"Keith," her tone grew more accusatory.

"See you tomorrow, Charlotte."

"Goodbye, Keith."

He disconnected the call and stared into space. Though he had waited all his life for this, he didn't feel happy. Particularly since Carl was petrified to marry him.

Winding up his arm in a parody of whipping the phone across the room in anger, Keith restrained himself and placed it back in its cradle.

Entering the bedroom, hearing the water from the shower in their private bath, Keith approached it, stepping into the steamy room.

Carl's blurry form was visible through the double glass doors. Gazing at him while he soaped up, Keith instantly felt his cock move in his jeans. Yes, Mark Richfield was pretty, and Steve Miller was macho, but nothing compared to Carl Bronson in his eyes.

Pushing back the door to peek in, Keith watched him lather up his chest and neck, eyes cast down, his hair sudsy from shampoo. Carl's young, thirty-year-old, tall, sleek, almost hairless torso made Keith salivate for a taste.

As if just realizing he had a visitor, Carl glanced up meeting Keith's eyes. "Hi."

"Hi," Keith crooned, taking off his shirt.

"Are you joining me?"

"Is that an invitation?" Keith kicked off his jeans and briefs.

"Yes," Carl laughed.

Pushing back the sliding door, Keith stepped into the blasting torrent. "I think I'm a sex fiend."

"Yeah?" Carl reached out for Keith and slid his soapy body around on him.

"Yes. Is that serious? Should I seek help?"

"Sea kelp?"

"What?" Keith squiggled against Carl's slick skin.

"Nothing. I'm making a joke that you didn't get."

"Hm?" Keith was already lost on Carl's body. Leaning back, using his fingers, Keith pressed their two hard, wet cocks together, rubbing them around each other.

"Nice." Carl held onto Keith's shoulders.

"I love the way that feels." Moving his palm over them, Keith glided up their stiff shafts happily. He arranged them to stand upright, getting a better grip.

"You going to jack us off?"

"Got a better idea?" Keith began panting as his hands moved faster.

As if Carl had just felt a zing of pleasure, he gulped, "No," then wrapped his fingers around Keith's.

With the two of them jerking up and down, Keith felt his balls tighten up. "Are you close?"

"Yes."

Carl's muscles hardened in his arms as they quickened the pace and slipped over the heads and down to the bases like a machine.

"I'm there…" Keith choked out the words as the rush began in his testicles.

"Oh, yes…" Carl opened his lips and closed his eyes. "Yes!"

A flood of creamy sperm squirted out of each slit, spattering their dripping wet skin and running down their clasped hands.

Before it was all washed away, Keith licked it off his hand, instantly bringing Carl's mouth to his to share the taste.

Carl's moan echoed off the wet tiles, making Keith's heart beat faster. Exchanging the tangy come between them, Keith wrapped tightly around Carl's waist, crushing him to his body. Why couldn't Carl marry him? Why couldn't they gather all their friends and family together to celebrate their love? Why?

~

Carl felt Keith's anguish even through his passion. No, their situation wasn't fair. But who ever said life was?

Parting from his kiss, Carl asked, "Are you done?"

"Let me just shampoo my hair."

After making sure he was soap free, Carl opened the door and grabbed a towel. Stepping out, he dried himself, staring as Keith finished up.

Marry you? I'd sell my soul to marry you. To wear your ring and vow my eternal love for you. But I can't. The world of Hollywood motion pictures won't let me.

Carl dabbed at his eye discreetly. After every lovely experience they shared, reality set in and they became maudlin. It sucked. This was supposed to be the best years of his and Keith's lives. They were young, still in their prime, successful, in love...hello? What else did you need for happiness?

What else?

Freedom.

And the one thing he and Keith did not have was freedom. Carl felt as if he was in a cage and the bars were electrified. Every time he reached out to the air outside the trap he was burned.

The water stopped. Drips from Keith's wet body to the porcelain tub replaced the sound of the spigot's rushing noise. The door moved back. Carl feasted his eyes on Keith's naked, drenched form. Twenty-six, blue-eyed, blond, the prettiest boy he ever did see. Mark excluded.

"Carl?"

Coming around from his daydream, seeing Keith rubbing a towel over his hair, Carl replied, "Yes?"

"Charlotte called while you were in the shower."

"And?" Carl flipped his wet towel over the glass door.

"She said the show did actually get six Emmy nominations."

Carl whipped his head around. "Are you kidding?"

"No. Including Best Lead and Supporting Actor in a Drama Series."

"Us?"

"Us."

"Not Omar?"

"No. Us."

Carl whooped in joy and picked Keith up out of the tub, spinning him around in excitement.

"Carl?"

Slowing down his pulse, Carl found Keith's expression did not reflect his own. He set Keith on his feet and asked, "What's wrong?"

"She wants us to come to the award ceremony as a couple."

"We can't do that."

"We have to. We promised her and the producers we wouldn't have more fake dates."

"No. That can't mean for the awards. We have to look straight for the awards."

"Carl," Keith implored.

In fury, Carl held up his hand. "Stop." He opened the bathroom door and stormed out.

"Please, Carl. This is about you and me, nothing else. I want to be with you."

Clenching his fists in agony, Carl cried, "Why does every good thing that happens to us have to be painted with the same brush of injustice? I can't stand this anymore."

Keith pressed his naked length against Carl's back, wrapping his arms around Carl's waist.

His anger deflating at the loving embrace, Carl overlapped Keith's arms and held him tight. "I'm sorry, Keith."

"I know, babe."

"I want to achieve the goal of a leading man in the movies."

"I know," Keith echoed softly.

Loosening Keith's hold, Carl spun around to face him and felt hot tears running down his cheeks. "I wish it didn't have to be this way."

"I understand. Carl, stop." Keith wiped at Carl's face.

"I love you. I'm proud of that love."

"Carl, stop crying. You'll get me started."

A sob broke from Carl's throat. He enfolded Keith in his arms and wept over his shoulder. "I'm sorry."

"Shh. It's okay."

"No. It isn't fucking okay."

Chapter Sixteen

After a fitful night's sleep, Carl felt rough. He was so fuzzy headed he cut his face shaving. Exiting the bathroom with toilet paper stuck to his chin, he scuffed his way to the kitchen where Keith had poured him a cup of coffee.

"You look like crap."

"I feel like crap." Carl dropped to a chair.

"You tossed and turned all night."

"I'm sorry. I should have slept in the other bedroom."

"Not on your life." Keith stood behind him and hugged his neck.

When the phone rang, Carl cringed. "Not this early."

"Maybe it's Mom." Keith checked the display. "Adam?"

"Uh oh. Mark." Carl flinched as if he were about to get slapped.

"Shit. You answer it."

"Me?"

"He'll kill me."

"Give me the phone." Carl reached out tiredly. "Hello?"

"Are you insane?" the voice on the other end asked.

"Good morning to you too, Adam." Carl rolled his eyes at Keith.

"Do you think flaunting your homosexuality is going to get you movie parts, Carl?"

"Flaunting? Who the hell is flaunting?" Carl cupped the

phone. "Go pick up the extension, he's going crazy."

Keith rushed to the bedroom.

Carl waited to hear Keith get on.

"Yes! Flaunting!"

Keith asked, "Are you talking about Mark?"

"Keith!" Adam roared, "You, Carl, and Mark are on the fucking cover of the *Inspirer*! Naked and in the same bed!"

"What?" Carl gasped. "Adam, that was from a shoot from the show we did yesterday. How the hell did they get it so quickly?"

"Off the net, Carl!" Adam yelled in fury.

"I knew it." Carl deflated.

"YouTube?" Keith asked sadly.

"Yes! What were you thinking getting Richfield involved in this?"

"Steve's okay with it," Keith said.

"Jack is going berserk!"

"Jack?" Carl replied. "What the heck does this have to do with Jack?"

"Forget that at the moment. What I want to know is, are you two outting yourselves to the public?"

"What did the article say, Adam?" Carl felt his temples pound with a headache.

As sarcastically as he could, Adam said, "Well, gee, boys, let me read you the headline, shall I?"

Carl held his breath.

"It says, '*Forever Young*'s Famous 'Straight'(and the word *straight* is in quotes, mind you,) Lovers Invite Gay Mate For a Day of Fun'. Shall I go on?"

Carl rubbed his eyes with his index finger and thumb creating dots of light under his eyelids.

"Adam…it was a shoot." Keith's loud sigh was heard over the line. "Charlotte wanted a threesome and we thought of Mark."

"Why? Why Mark? What the hell's wrong with you? Couldn't Charlotte cast a straight man? For Christ's sake, where do you want your careers to be after this show ends?"

"Adam, your shouting is giving me a headache," Carl moaned.

"You want to know what the headache will be, Carl? Me finding either one of you work after the finale. Okay? That's the fucking headache."

"Please stop yelling at us, Adam. Carl and I are already miserable."

After a long silence where Carl could only hear breathing, Adam whispered, "Just come out. Come the fuck out."

"I can't," Carl whined.

"Carl, you have to. You're completely outted as it is, and denying it like I once advised you will make you both look like the biggest fucking liars in the country."

"Kiss my film career goodbye?" Carl choked up.

"Take your chances."

Carl set the phone down and covered his face to cry.

Over the line he heard Keith calling his name. "Carl?" A second later Keith rushed in to comfort him. "Adam, I have to go, Carl's a mess. Fine. I'll call you tonight. Bye."

Keith disconnected both phones.

Curled in a ball over his lap, Carl was in agony. As Keith coaxed him into his arms, Carl wailed like a baby, letting out all his anger and frustration.

"Shh...oh, Carl. Please...stop crying." Keith hiccupped and began to weep with him. "I love you. I can't take seeing you like this. We'll be okay. Please."

His body racked with sobs as he wept, Carl had lost all strength to keep fighting. Everyone wanted them exposed for what they were.

But what were they? Weren't they just two people in love?

"Carl," Keith bawled with him and Carl knew it was Keith seeing him so upset that was making Keith cry.

Struggling to get a hold of himself, Carl swallowed down his hurt pride and kissed Keith's salty cheek. "Okay, babe. Okay."

"I'm sorry," Keith wailed. "I did this. I invited Mark, I suggested the threesome to Charlotte. Hate me, Carl. I've ruined your career. Hate me."

"No. Never." Carl held Keith's head in his hands and kissed his teary face. "It's not you. It's the powers that be who make the decision that a person's sexual lifestyle affects his talent. It's not you, Keith. Please. Never blame yourself."

"But I'm forcing you out when you don't want to be."

"Hush. Stop. We actually have to work today and we're both a shambles." Carl dabbed at Keith's eyes. "And you're wrong. I want to be out. Are you kidding me? I hate hiding, lying, feeling like a damn convict. What's our crime, Keith?"

Keith dove on Carl and wrapped around him in a vice grip.

"Shh, okay. We'll be all right." Carl knew once *Forever Young* was through, so were they. It was time to scrimp and save. And they had better make damn sure this series went for a decade.

Chapter Seventeen

Camera flashed. Fans screamed.

The noise and commotion was distracting. Carl's hand was squeezed tight. He waved at the shrieking men and women and was surprised to see quite a few rainbow banners. Media people with omnipresent microphones snatched the stars for comments and questions.

"Carl Bronson! Carl Bronson!"

Carl noticed a popular television station logo on a black microphone as he was waved over. A loud roar from the spectators exploded from his advance.

"Carl, you must be very excited to be nominated for your first leading television role."

"I am. It's very thrilling."

"Keith?" The man with the microphone urged him closer. "And you, a newcomer to the business. How do you feel?"

After a shy smile, Keith replied, "Exhilarated. It's like a crazy rollercoaster ride."

"I notice the two of you holding hands. Are you finally making a statement?"

Carl smiled at Keith. "We are."

"You are two very brave men. I wish you luck."

"Thank you." Carl waved at the screaming fans, tightening his grip on Keith's hand. He paused as several photographers took their picture. Carl felt his stomach fluttering like a camera shutter, but pretended he was confident.

"You okay?" Keith asked softly.

"Yes. I want to be here with you. Like this."

"I love you."

Carl gave his lover an endearing smile.

They were shown to a table in the grand Governor's Ballroom. It was like a who's who of A-list Hollywood celebrities. Carl felt odd to be among them.

As they passed, several big named male movie stars winked in approval. Carl felt slightly bitter that he and Keith were making a stand while so many others were deathly afraid. But he understood. He sympathized with their plight.

Finding the cast, producers, writers, and of course, Charlotte and her husband already there, Carl released Keith's hand to hug her and their co-stars Cheryl Jones and Betty Blue who were also nominated.

"Well done, boys." Derek Dixon was seated with his beautiful wife while Will Markham was accompanied by his handsome partner, Madison Henning. Carl smiled in pride to see Will not behaving like a hypocrite. "Thank you, Mr. Dixon."

"How's it feel?" Will asked eagerly.

"Scary as hell."

"You won't feel that way with that hot little trophy in your hands."

"If we win," Keith mentioned softly.

"You will." Will and Derek winked at them as if they knew something that Carl and Keith didn't.

"Are you coming to the ceremony after?" Keith asked the group.

"Wouldn't miss it for the world." Charlotte kissed Keith's cheek, leaving a lipstick mark which she rubbed off with her thumb.

~

The evening felt very long and tiring as all the small awards for art direction and production went first. Keith stifled a yawn, hoping he wasn't being filmed for the television audience at that moment.

Finally the announcements were made for their categories. Best Supporting Actor in a Drama Series came first. Keith sat up in his seat as clips were played on a big screen of each candidate.

"Good luck, babe." Carl held Keith's hand.

Suddenly Carl was screaming and Charlotte was jumping up and down.

"Did I win?"

"Yes! Go get your award!" Carl laughed.

"Really? They said my name?"

Charlotte stood, grabbed Keith's hand, and got him to his feet, pushing on his bottom to move him in the right direction. The audience went wild with hilarity at her actions.

A buzz from the noise in his ears making him dizzy, Keith made it to the stairs and stage, but couldn't think. He was on autopilot. His tuxedo-clad image was being broadcast on large screens all over the stage. The famous male star holding his trophy grinned knowingly at him. Keith felt as if he was suddenly accepted into a secret club and all the closeted gay men in Hollywood were looking at him with admiration and envy at being out.

"Thank you," Keith said as he took the statue. He was left alone at a podium. Instantly, all he could see was Carl. He held it up to him. "For you, babe. For you. I couldn't have done it without you. Oh, and Charlotte." Keith laughed at himself. Holding the statue up high, he waved, "Thank you."

Having no idea what else to say, he walked away from the microphone and was escorted back to his seat. Once he plopped down in his chair and set the idol on the table, he opened his mouth to Carl in a gape and said, "I can't believe it."

"I can." Carl grabbed Keith's hand and rubbed it in his.

Everyone around him reached to congratulate him.

Only a moment later the Lead Actor in a Drama Series was being announced.

Keith stared at Carl as they said his name and showed a clip of the show. Keith wanted Carl to win so badly he would die if Carl didn't.

Yet another top sexy Hollywood leading man stood with the envelope. To Keith's amazement, before the man opened the flap he looked directly at Carl. Keith knew right at that moment Carl had won.

"And the winner is...Carl Bronson from *Forever Young.*"

"Carl!" Keith shouted in excitement.

"Come with me." Carl yanked Keith's arm.

"What?" Keith choked in shock. Looking back at his producers and his director, he found them waving him on.

As Keith rose to his feet with Carl, the audience went crazy. There was no lack of support in front of the camera for them. It was behind the scenes that was the brutal reality.

Carl released Keith's hand as they closed in on the handsome movie star who handed Carl his award. Once he had, Carl reached back for Keith. Keith was standing shyly behind him, more nervous than when he received his own statue. At Carl's insistence, Keith stood next to him, feeling Carl's hand wrap warmly around his waist.

"Thank you." Carl held the award up. "To the producers, Derek Dixon and Will Markham who steered me in the right direction. To Charlotte Deavers whose constant creative genius astounds me. To my co-stars who are infinitely talented and inspire me. To all the fans who watch the show and make it what it is." Carl gave Keith a demonic grin that made Keith's knees wobble. "And to Keith O'Leary. My strength, my support, my guiding force, and my lover."

When Carl kissed him, Keith blinked in shock and had to hold onto Carl to prevent fainting.

Once he had parted from Keith's lips, Carl waved the statue at the roaring crowd and held Keith around the waist as they were led off the stage.

The comedian MC returned to the microphone. "Another first for Emmy night. The first gay kiss. I hope the censors keep it in. Well done, men!"

Carl sat down again, staring at Keith with a big wild grin on his face.

"You are amazing," Keith laughed in awe.

"Get over here." Carl grabbed him and planted a good, wet tongue kiss on him. When Keith peeked up, it was being broadcast on the big screens behind the host.

"Now, now, boys," the comedian teased, "you're liable to coax others out of the closet with that behavior."

Carl roared with laughter and held Keith tight. "I love you."

"I love you to, you sexy thing," Keith purred. Seeing Charlotte's proud smile, Keith didn't know how their night could get any better. But it would. The best was yet to come.

Chapter Eighteen

On the beach in Malibu with the choppy Pacific Ocean at their backs, the September light beginning to wane, Carl stood next to Keith, surrounded by all their friends and co-workers.

Still high from the award ceremony, Carl held Keith's hand tightly as a private photographer took photos.

A Justice of the Peace stood with an opened book in his hand in front of the happy couple. "Repeat after me. I, Carl Bronson, take you Keith O'Leary to be my husband, my partner in life, and my one true love."

Carl gazed into Keith's teary blue eyes. "I, Carl Bronson, take you Keith O'Leary to be my husband, my partner in life, and my one true love."

"I will cherish our friendship and love you today, tomorrow, and forever. I will trust you and honor you, I will laugh with you and cry with you."

Carl choked up, trying to keep his voice strong. "I will cherish our friendship and love you today, tomorrow, and forever. I will trust you and honor you, I will laugh with you and cry with you."

"I will love you faithfully through the best and the worst, through the difficult and the easy. What may come, I will always be there."

Dabbing at his eyes, Carl repeated, "I will love you faithfully through the best and the worst, through the difficult and the easy. What may come, I will always be there."

"As I have given you my hand to hold so I give you my life to keep. So help me God."

"As I have given you my hand to hold so I give you my life to keep. So help me God." The last syllable cracked from the emotion Carl felt.

As Keith repeated the same vows back to him, tears ran from Carl's eyes.

The Justice of the Peace asked, "Both of you repeat after me. Entreat me not to leave you, or to return from following after you, for where you go I will go, and where you stay I will stay."

Struggling with his words, Carl heard Keith's voice quivering as well. "Entreat me not to leave you, or to return from following after you, for where you go I will go, and where you stay I will stay."

"And where you die, I will die, and there I will be buried. May the Lord do with me and more if anything but death parts you from me."

Unable to contain it, Carl was sobbing he was so happy. "And where you die, I will die, and there I will be buried. May the Lord do with me and more if anything but death parts you from me."

"Do you have the rings?"

Mark handed Carl a gold band. Carl slipped it on Keith's finger.

Adam gave Keith one next.

Keith pushed it on Carl with trembling hands.

"By the power invested in my in the state of California, I now pronounce you husband and husband."

Keith pounced on Carl and kissed him, almost knocking him over. Carl wrapped around him and lifted him off his feet.

They were showered with rose petals as they raced into

Adam's Malibu home.

"I love you, husband." Keith giggled like he was drunk.

"I love you too, *husband*!" Carl broke up with laughter.

As the crowd filtered into the home, popping champagne bottles sounded in every direction.

Adam raised a glass. "To two very brave, wonderful men!"

The crowd agreed, tapping glasses.

Carl kept kissing Keith. The feeling of being married to Keith thrilled him.

"Can I kiss the bride?"

Carl found Mark's luscious smile. Both he and Keith dove on Mark and dipped him precariously backwards as they chewed on his neck and lips.

When Mark was set back upright he appeared completely woozy. "Wow."

Carl broke up with laughter and grabbed his husband again. "I love you. You know that?"

"Even though we may be out of work in five years?"

"Yes. Even though. Screw it. I can direct."

"And I can do gay porn."

Carl caught Keith's impish smile and held him tight. While they teased each other with the tips of their tongues dueling, Charlotte shouted, "Perfect for next season! Your wedding and honeymoon night."

"She's a horny lady."

"I know. Lucky us." Keith hugged him, locking onto his lips once more.

Pulling the men closer to her, Charlotte whispered, "Can I confide a secret to you both?"

Carl felt his skin tingle at her serious tone. "What is it, Charlotte?"

Laughing, Keith asked, "Are you coming out, Charlotte?"

"No. Sweetie, I have a confession to make."

"Oh?" Carl felt the smile fall from his face.

"It was me who leaked the story to the press and set up the YouTube site. Will you ever forgive me?"

"You?" Keith pointed at her.

"Yes. Derek and Will were putting a huge amount of pressure on me for the February sweeps. Please forgive me."

Carl met Keith's eyes. "What choice do we have? If we don't forgive you, we're out of work."

"No. That won't happen. If it was up to me, the show would go on like a soap, for twenty years."

"Oh, Charlotte," Keith sighed sadly. "You caused us a lot of grief."

"I'm sorry, boys. Honest. But in reality, didn't it help you get here?" She gestured to the party. "To coming out and getting married?"

Carl thought about it. There was some truth to her words. Without all the devious tactics, he and Keith would still be hiding. What would happen to their future careers was still up for debate.

"I forgive you," Carl sighed.

"Me too, Charlotte."

"I love you both, you know that?"

"Group hug!" Keith laughed as she embraced them.

"It'd be group sex if Charlotte has her way," Carl laughed.

"Oh?" Charlotte's eyes sparkled, "Oh, Mark..." she sang. "Mr. Richfield?"

"Bad girl!" Carl admonished.

"I can dream, can't I?"

"Go to your husband. You're making him jealous." Keith nudged her.

After she walked away, Carl drew Keith against him. "We thought it was her."

"Yes. Ratings mean more to Charlotte than anything."

"Forget it. It's meaningless now." Carl kissed him.

"I love you, Mr. O'Leary." Keith grinned slyly.

"What? Aren't you, Mr. Bronson?"

"Who cares, kiss me."

Carl wrapped around him tight and sucked at his mouth. A cheer of applause rang out around them. That was the kind of feedback Carl craved for he and Keith. A standing ovation.

Turn the page for a look at:

Getting It In The End

Book Three of the Action! Series

By G.A. Hauser

Coming in March 2009
Brought to you by Linden Bay Romance

Chapter One

Changing into their shorts and t-shirts, Steve stared at Mark as he sat down on their bed to yank on a pair of socks.

"It's hot out. You want to just do a quick three miles?"

"That doesn't sound like very much." Steve stood, tucking in his shirt.

"Four?"

"Okay. Four. We'll save the long runs for the weekend."

"It's too bloody hot out." Mark found a rubber band and pulled his long hair back from his face.

Steve loved to ogle him. Just the sight of Mark Richfield put him in heat. And now that he and Mark were running every day together, Steve looked forward to the sweaty after-run sex that followed the exercise. It was their daily routine.

He thought he'd tire of Mark, working at the same advertising agency and living with him. But that never happened. At work they soon were immersed in separate deals and rarely caught up until the drive home, so it didn't seem as if they were overlapping to the extreme.

Once Mark had his LA Dodgers ball cap in place, his long brown ponytail flowing out of the back, Steve couldn't resist. Wrapping around his narrow waist, he swung Mark to his chest, and contacted his mouth.

Grinding his hips into Mark's, feeling that big dick of his rubbing against him, even when it wasn't fully erect, Steve lit on fire.

Parting from the kiss, Mark chided, "Officer Miller. If you keep that up, the sex won't wait until after the run."

"Sorry, I couldn't resist." Steve forced himself to let go. Something that was harder than his cock at the moment.

"Right. Shall we?" Mark led the way out of their bedroom while Steve salivated at the sight of his tight ass in tiny red shorts.

Once they were running at their normal pace, Mark said, "Oh, I forgot to mention something to you."

"Yes, dear?" Steve asked playfully as they ran passed rows of stately homes with gated entries.

"You know that silly new account, Artists and Models for Hire?"

"You mean that front for prostitution?"

"Steven! It isn't a front for prostitution." Mark paused at a corner and tapping Steve to go when the cars cleared out.

"Sure it ain't."

"You think Parsons and Company would take their account if they weren't strictly above board?"

"Never mind. What about them, Mark?"

"Well, when I went there to talk them into some long term advertising, the owner, Arnold Newhouse, just about begged me to do a photo shoot."

Steve groaned in annoyance. "I thought you were dead set against modeling, Mark."

"Well, I am."

"But?"

"I just thought it might be a pleasant diversion. I wouldn't take anything seriously. And after that little guest spot I did on *Forever Young* with Carl Bronson and Keith O'Leary, I have to admit I got a taste of it and I liked it."

"Vanity, vanity…" Steve teased.

"Are you running deliberately fast to lose me?"

"To punish you." Steve gave him a sly glance.

"Stop it or I'll leave you in the dust."

Steve slowed down slightly knowing Mark was much faster in a sprint than he was. "So? Now you suddenly want to model? Is this a career change, or in addition to Parsons and Co.?"

"No. Not a career change. I just thought it might be good for a laugh."

"You're jealous of Angel Loveday."

"Oh, shut up. You do say the most unbelievable things."

"I just don't understand this sudden need to be photographed."

"I did it before. You remember that male nude coffee table book? *American Male-Men*?"

"Yes, though I've never seen it. How could I forget? Larsen has like ten copies."

"Two. He has two."

"Look, you want me to take some naked shots of you, stick them on the web and expose your nice big cock for you?"

"Shut up, Steven."

"Hey, now look who's increasing the pace! Slow the fuck down or we'll never make it four miles."

"I didn't say they would be pornographic. Why do you have such a demented mind?"

"Because I've seen you naked, and if I were to take photos of you, they'd be showing your lusciously large male anatomy."

"Not all models show off their privates. I was thinking more of headshots anyway." Mark adjusted the brim of his cap over his sunglasses in the glare.

"Look, you do what you like. If you think it'll be fun, go for it."

"Thank you. That's all I wanted to hear."

When Mark felt Steve's hand on his ass, he twisted back to look at him in exasperation. "You're trying to make me trip."

"No, I'm trying to cop a feel."

"You'll get your feel later, copper."

"Mmm, can't fucking wait."

Mark laughed at him as the pace began to get more grueling.

~

Mark couldn't breathe they were running so hard. As they neared their home on the last leg of their run they tended to race to the finish. After four miles of boiling heat and a pace much faster than Mark would have liked, Steve bolted to the front of the house, competitive in every way.

Letting up before they both smacked into the front door to 'tag' the finish line, Mark halted, allowing Steve to slap the wood and 'win'. Leaning over his knees, Mark gasped for air as the sweat dripped down his body and into his eyes.

"Son of a bitch, it's hot." Steve groaned, untying his key from his shoelace.

Taking off his cap and sunglasses Mark mopped up his face with his drenched t-shirt. "You always have to make it into a competition."

"I have to be better than you at something, Richfield." Steve pushed back the door and they both groaned with relief at the air-conditioned coolness.

Heading to the refrigerator, Mark removed two bottles of water, handing one to Steve and gulping his. Finally able to breathe normally, Mark took off his shirt to use to soak up the sweat that continued to pour out of him as he cooled down.

Steve flicked his tongue over Mark's exposed nipple.

Raising his eyebrow at the gesture, Mark inspected the demonic expression on his lover's face. "Give me a minute. I'm not twenty any longer."

"Maybe not, but you have the body of a twenty year old." Steve wrapped around Mark, licking the slow moving drops of sweat from Mark's chest. "And you weren't too old for an orgy with Keith and Carl."

"Oh, that," Mark moaned, remembering he and Steve having a four-way sexual romp with the two hottest stars on cable television. "I think my multiple-partner days are over. It was fun, but…"

"But?" Steve sucked one of Mark's nipples, biting it between his lip-covered teeth.

"I just want you, Officer Miller. I think thirty-seven is too old to be playing around like that."

Leaning back, Steve asked, "Really?"

"Yes, love. Really." Mark finished the water in his bottle and tossed it into the kitchen sink. Steve had his arms wrapped around Mark's waist, preventing him from going anywhere.

"Is that why you want to do this modeling thing?" Steve asked. "Because you feel as if you're getting older?"

Hating to admit it, Mark lowered his eyelashes. "I won't be attractive forever, Steve. And once I'm old, what will be left of me but memories of my looks?"

Parting from him, Steve raised Mark's chin up so he would meet his eyes. "There's more to you than your beauty, Mark."

Laughing sadly, Mark replied, "Sure there is. And you would have been attracted to my personality if I looked different."

"Cut this shit out." Steve shook him. "Do you think I'm that shallow that all I wanted you for was your body?"

Mark instantly met Steve's blue eyes. A sharp pain seared through Mark's chest. He knew he was an emotional mess. If it wasn't for his sex appeal, he'd be alone.

"Mark?"

"Let me shower. I'm hot." Turning away from Steve's irritated expression, Mark climbed the stairs to their bedroom. He stood next to their bed, shedding the rest of his clothing and leaving it in a damp pile for the laundry basket. Hearing Steve undressing behind him, Mark stepped into the bathroom. Before he turned on the shower he peeked at the mirror.

The first thing he found was his eyes. Bright green irises framed by long, dark thick lashes. Taking the rubber band out of his hair, he combed through its damp, sweaty length, feeling it brush the nape of his neck and shoulders.

With both palms he leaned on the sink and stared critically at his features. He'd been compared to a woman his whole life; called pretty, fag, androgynous, Ganymede, and everything under the sun to slam whatever was left of his manhood. His father was abusive. Being an only child, Mark had to bear the brunt of all Milt Richfield's anger and frustration. No matter what Mark had achieved, his dominating father never saw fit to praise him. It wasn't Mark's fault his mother was a cold fish. Why was he to blame for all the spats between his parents?

Mark leaned on his best friend Jack Larsen for support all through college. Though he put up a front of confidence, Mark was insecure and weak, relying on the men in his life for the strength he needed.

Steve appeared in the mirror's reflection. As he wrapped around Mark from behind, looking at him from over his shoulder in the glass, Mark met his loving light eyes.

"What's going on, Mark?" Steve rocked him gently.

Biting his lip as he fought for a way to explain how he felt, Mark exhaled a deep breath first. "Steven. I feel like Dorian Gray. That everything I've done in my life will turn me into what I really am inside."

"And what are you inside?" Steve kissed Mark's neck.

"Ugly."

Steve urged Mark around so they were facing each other. Mark felt the press of Steve's hot genitals against his own.

"You are not ugly, Mark. Far from it. You're loving, kind, and sweet."

"You're biased because you are attracted to my looks."

"What's brought all this on?" Steve toyed with the long tresses of Mark's hair.

"There's too much going through my mind at the moment."

"Can I help? Do you want to talk about it?"

"No." Mark attempted to break the embrace to get to the shower. Steve held him firm.

"Why do I get the feeling this is all coming on the heels of that sex we had with Keith and Carl?"

It was. Steve had it dead on. What Steve did not know, was that he had a three-way with those men the day before they all got together. In other words, he cheated on Steve only to bring him in on the event later to appease his guilt. Not only that, but Keith O'Leary had manipulated Steve to allow Mark to do a guest appearance on their late night cable television drama, *Forever Young*.

The shame was beginning to gnaw at Mark. And that didn't even begin to open up the dam of emotion of what all of this playing around had done to his best friend, Jack Larsen.

Mark was furious with himself. Ego. Ego and pride had once again led Mark down the wrong path. And now he was living to regret it.

"Mark?"

"Let me shower." Mark reached into the stall and turned on the taps. Feeling Steve running kisses down his neck and shoulders, Mark bit back the tears knowing he didn't deserve a man as wonderful as Steven Jay Miller.

~

Waiting his turn as Mark wet down under the spraying head, Steve pulled leisurely on his own cock as it grew excited. Looking at Mark, his tall sleek body, his bronze flawless skin and large male anatomy, soft, and hanging low between his legs, Steve salivated. Yes, Mark's looks were a complete turn-on, but if Mark was nasty and conceited, those looks would mean nothing. Mark Antonious Richfield was as soft and voluptuous as a woman on the inside. Feline eyes and movements, long thick shiny hair, and the biggest dick Steve had ever seen on a man, Mark was everything Steve wanted and more. Kneeling, Steve opened his lips and allowed Mark's soft penis into his mouth. The water from the shower ran down Mark's golden skin and against Steve's face.

As Steve drew Mark's cock completely inside him, it pulsated and grew. Closing his eyes to the pelting water, Steve wrapped his right hand around Mark's hips and toyed with his heavy sack with his other.

A low groan echoed around the wet tiles. Steve knew once Mark was completely erect he wouldn't be able to fit him entirely inside his mouth. He never could get all of it in no matter how he tried. Steve had an image flash of Keith O'Leary, that sexy blue-eyed blond superstar sucking Mark's cock and Carl Bronson, Keith's muscular brunette co-star, enveloping Mark's balls. All while Steve clasped his hands at the base of Mark's penis at the same time to make Mark shiver and come. Just thinking about it caused Steve to whimper in excitement and his dick to bob in yearning.

Those two handsome actors wanted Mark so badly they seduced Steve just so he would agree. And the image of Mark on his hands and knees taking it up the ass from him and sucking

Keith's dick at the same time was an image Steve would never forget.

Moaning louder than Mark from his carnal thoughts and cravings, Steve gripped the base of Mark's long shaft in two hands and drew as hard as he could on it to the tip, sliding it as deeply as he dared into his throat. He tasted Mark's pre-come nectar of the gods, on his tongue. So few had the privilege of having sex with this man, Steve knew he was lucky to have found him. He stole Mark away from Sharon Tice. Snatched Mark from the altar of their wedding day- mid-vows. And now Mark was his. Not Jack's, not Sharon's, not Keith's, nor Carl's, but his.

And Steve was as possessive as a dog with his favorite bone over this man. Possessive and defensive. As an ex-LAPD cop, Steve wanted to protect and serve one man, till his death.

That throaty gasp of Mark's always sent shivers down Steve's spine. Increasing his speed and suction, Steve reached between Mark's legs and found his tight ring, pushing in.

Those delicious whimpering cries, *Ah! Ah*! sent Steve wild. A vibrating throbbing rattled Mark's long cock and Steve began swallowing down the load. Groaning, closing his eyes tighter at the taste and quantity of Mark's come, Steve could live on his knees before this man and be happy.

~

Bracing himself on the tile and shower door, Mark felt the reverberation of the orgasm rock his body. Before he could recover, Steve had spun him to face the wall, shoving his dick up his ass. Mark closed his eyes as Steve's soapy cock slid in deep and fast. Shivering at the penetration, loving Steve's body inside his, Mark went numb from the overload to his senses. This macho tough guy knew what he wanted. An alpha male in every way,

Steve was the top to Mark's bottom exclusively. And Mark would have it no other way.

He loved getting it in the end, loved it. And playing submissive to this amazing masculine ex-cop was pure fantasy. Why he would do anything to jeopardize it, Mark didn't know.

It didn't take long. With Steve, it rarely did. Mark remembered Steve's conversations in the dark, how he used to learn tricks to hold back so he could please Sonja Knight, his ex-attorney girlfriend. It didn't matter anymore. Steve could spurt in one second. Mark didn't need him to stay hard to come, not like a woman. Though saying that, Mark didn't want Steve to pull out either. The heat, the connection, and the unity, made Mark feel whole. When Steve was inside him, Mark felt worthy.

As Steve's thrusting hips slapped Mark's wet bottom, Steve's hands gripped Mark's flaccid cock. Steve climaxed. Hearing Steve's deep grunting, feeling Steve's weight nail him to the wall, Mark closed his eyes. It was the only time he was at peace.

Gently, Steve disconnected from Mark's body, holding Mark's hips as he did.

"I love you," Steve hissed seductively.

Smiling, Mark always heard an 'I love you' after Steve fucked him. Maybe it was Steve's way of thanking him.

As a tease, Mark replied, "You're welcome."

There was no jovial laugh in response. Steve urged Mark to turn around. When Mark did, he found anguish in Steve's expression. He wasn't prepared for that. "What did I do now?"

"Nothing. Get over here." Steve embraced him, kissing Mark deeply, his tongue hard inside Mark's mouth like a miniature cock. When Steve parted from Mark's lips he whispered, "Don't worry. Whatever it is you're thinking about. Don't let it upset you."

Smiling at his hero, his savior, Mark whispered back, "I do love you. You know that."

Steve gripped Mark's jaw roughly, making Mark look at him. "I know."

About the Author:

Award-winning author G. A. Hauser was born in Fair Lawn, New Jersey, and attended university in New York City. She moved to Seattle, Washington, where she worked as a patrol officer with the Seattle Police Department. In early 2000 G.A. moved to Hertfordshire, England, where she began her writing in earnest and published her first book, *In the Shadow of Alexander*. Now a full-time writer in Ohio, G.A. has written dozens of novels, including several bestsellers of gay fiction. For more information on other books by G.A., visit the author at her official website at: www.authorga.com.

Other works by G.A. Hauser:

This is a publication of
Linden Bay Romance
WWW.LINDENBAYROMANCE.COM

Printed in the United Kingdom by
Lightning Source UK Ltd., Milton Keynes
140407UK00001B/10/P